IN MY HOOD

ENDY

http://www.melodramapublishing.com

In My 'Hood
Copyright © 2006 by Endy Greene

For information address:
Melodrama Publishing
P. O. Box 522
Bellport, New York 11713-0522
646-879-6315

Web address: www.melodramapublishing.com
e-mail: melodramapub@aol.com
author's email address: **Edimples@aol.com**
Library of Congress Control Number: 2005936568
ISBN 0-9717021-9-5
First Edition

This novel is a work of fiction. Any resemblances to actual events, real people, living or dead, organizations, establishments, locales are prod-ucts of the author's imagination. Other names, characters, places, and incidents are used fictitiously.

10 9 8 7 6 5 4 3 2 1
First Paperback Edition

IN MY HOOD

ACKNOWLEDGMENTS

First and foremost I'd like to thank my Lord and savior Jesus Christ from whom all blessing flow. Without Him I am nothing, but with Him I can do all things!

I know that a lot of you will be reading this only to see if your name appears. I want to let those people know that your name does not have to be in print for me to show you my appreciation. If you don't see your name, charge it to my head not my heart, because my heart is truly innocent. Just know this is to acknowledge the people that are active in my life now. Those who've encouraged and supported me to move on with this project. But that doesn't mean those of you I didn't mention are less meaningful in my life. I'll get you on the next go round.

I like to start off by thanking my mother Francis. Mommy you are my world, my friend and my advisor. You have helped me way beyond belief. Your patience with me is overwhelming for days when I had no patience. I will pass all of your knowledge and strength down to my own daughters. There are not enough words in the dictionary to describe the love and appreciation I hold for you. Oh yeah, you still can't read this book. (smile)

Next I'd like to give thanks to my father George (Georgie). Your strength and strict values have taught me the meaning of life. They have taught me how to be a strong woman. They have taught me to be aware of my surroundings and not to hold low standards of myself as a woman. I know I have to work for what I want. I know one thing because of you I know how to get my grind on. You are definitely the GRIND MASTER! Legally that is.

To my beautiful daughters, Briona and Len-da. Mommy loves you so much! You are my life, the air that I breathe and the blood that runs through my veins. We did it girls! Mommy finally finished. I want to thank you for your encouragement and for your patience. I am so proud of both of you for the way you gave me my space to complete this project. Even though it took a lot of time from you, you knew that it was important to me and you constantly encouraged me. I love you more than life for that. Let me find out that both my daughters are fierce with the pen. Keep pumping out those short stories girls! I see ya' work with the sketching thing too. Anything is possible when you work hard at it.

To my brother Dariane, thank you for helping me with the girls while I completed this project. I am so proud of you! I knew you could do it! I love you! You are the best Uncle to the girls and the best brother a sister can ever have!

To my dear Aunt Lillian. Thank you for your genuine kindness. Thank you for taking me and treating me like I was your own child. It is a blessing to be related to you.

Tondalaya (Tondie) my cuz'n, thank you for being right there with me every step of the way. Even though you harassed me to get this project done! Just playing, that is exactly what I needed to get a move on. Thanks Cuz! ….Tamiko (Miko) what up fam'? Thank you so much for your encouragement, your support, friendship and for your crazy since of humor. Keep it straight Grimey! Yo…You hear the music? I think I hear it too. Hey Destiny!….To my girl Princess (P-Nice), Thank you so much for being there for me and my daughters in times of need. I can truly say you are a friend that I can count on. Hey Brianna, Nadia and Nina! What's up Rick? ….Hak thank you so much for your support, help and feed back. Thank you for your honesty and your crazy ass sense of humor, don't change a thing.

I'd like to thank DJ Ta-Rod (Lenny) for helping to create two of the most precious children a mother and father can have. Even though you get on my damn nerves at times!…lmao… You will always have a special place in my heart. You still my nigga! (Ay yo, they just don't get it! You feel me right? Night-night!)

Dorothy Stokes I appreciate your constant encouragement and the genuine love you've shown me. Thank you for all that you've done, I needed it. I know it was hard for you to do sometimes. But your heart is genuine. I love you! ….Daddy Mack! What's good? We miss you! Call us!….I ain't forget you Aunt Ree. I Love you too!

Michelle (Shelley) thank you for being a **true** friend. For reminding me that I'm a beautiful person when I needed to be reminded. For bringing the brighter side to any bad situation. We Libra's got to stick together, right? Thank you again for just being the beautiful person that you are! God is good! Luv you my sista!….Sonya (Sonnie) thank you for being there for me when I needed it. For your honesty and the many laughs we shared together along with those bangin' ass times all of us had turning the clubs out diva style! You are a great friend. I love you!……Hey Cynt (Fry Lady) What's up girl?….Hey Kim G. God is good girl! What's up my spiritual sista?

Hey Len-nette, I peeped how nice you are with the pen flow too. So what you waiting for? You will always be my daughter. Thanks for playing the *nice* big sister. Luv ya!……..What's good Monica? We been through a lot together thanks for being there……To my son Ta-Rod Jr. (TJ) Keep your head in those books and make me proud! Luv ya!

Hey Stephanie (Stevie), wake up! (smile) Thanks for the long conversation that we had on the phone about life. (Even though you fell asleep on me at times.) You are one sister I admire and will always respect. The courage and strength you have blows me away. Just your life alone is a best selling book! I'm drinking milk everyday so when I grow up I can to be just like you! Luv you!….Dennis, what's good man. Thanks for keeping it real and for not turning your back on me no matter what was going on. You will always be my brother-in-law….Billy (Unc) you know you my dogg, right? You always had me and the girls' best interest at heart. Thank you so much!

Anita (Nit) thanks for the many laughs we shared. Thanks for bringing a brighter side to all the Pop Warner drama! I'll meet you at the dollar bar!….Hey Shawnette! Where you at? Holla at your girl! You know I gotcha back! Just say when cause I'm down for the title! Hold me down baby!…. Chonda thanks for reaching out to me making sure our children who share the same blood stay and grow up together as family! That is so important to me. When I met you I knew we where sisters from another mother in another time all along. All good things come to those who wait. Luv you Sister!…..To my peeps Rennie (L) What's good man? You are one funny dude, stay just as you are and the world will be at your mercy. You know you special to get this, right? To my Boo Dante, what's good babe? Thank you for keeping my spirits up while workin at that dead beat company. You know you my n-gga! Luv you!

To my family just to name a few. Barbara hey big cuz! Thank you for the many laughs….Roscoe (nicest trumpet player around) I'm hungry when you cooking out? ……Alice I need a cake baked right about now, I'll be there to get it….Hey Cookie….Danaia (Netay) give my sweetheart Ian a kiss for me. (kiss-kiss) You are truly an original cuz, don't ever change....What's up Anniese, Brian, Felicia...Hey Shawn you hungry? I am......Hey Aunt Ann and Uncle Jimmy ....Charles (Chaz) I know the next time I look up you will be the owner and founder of a multi billion dollar company. Yo cuz you got the drive for it!.... Family thank you for having faith in me when doing this project. See y'all at the next family party! Ay...Yo...Aight! (You know how we do it!) Step in the name of love! One...Two...

Tracey, Lakeeda & Sadeeka Hot-Lanta ladies. I love yall so much! I miss y'all!.....I want to say what's up to all my family representing the dirty south. Just to name a few Bridgett, Melissa, Ann. All my aunts, uncles and cousins in Georgia. Florida: my aunts Carrie, Phyllis, Trish, Tina and Angela and everybody else!......Hey Rokisha (Ro) I didn't forget you. I'm glad you and I became friends. You are a real and beautiful woman. Our friendship will last an eternity. Hey Bridette and Brinae! I miss yall. Bri who's doing your hair? It better be tight!

They say people come into your life at a certain time for a reason. **Ty Goode** I want to thank you so much for your help and support. Your kindness is unforgettable. I wish you nothing but the best of luck with your books **Sinful Desires** and **His Baggage Her Load**. Always remember keep God first and everything else will fall into place. What's up with the sequel? (Smile)

Adrianne, what's up? I'm a published author! Thank you so much Adrianne for all your support. Thank you for your sincere friendship and kindness. Hey Toria, Tara, Trevor Jr. and Trevor Sr.! ...I want to give special thanks to Katie Tucker. Thank you for remembering me. This book may not have been possible without your memory. You are indeed a wonderful person!

Janice, I bet you thought I forgot you? Not happening. Now you know I owe a bunch of thank you's to you. You always have my back even when I don't realize you're there. When I look up, there you are. Thank you a thousand times over. You are the true meaning of long distance friends. Yeah... that's right I was sitting pretty up in that car! Hi Steph and Jaeda.....What's up Linden Pop Warner?.....Felicia and Diane Goode What's up? Thank you so much for blowin' my big ass head up bigger then it already is. Thanks for keeping it gully with me. Ay Fe....my head is still hurting from those braids you put in 7 months ago. (smile)....I didn't forget you Shakira. Thank you for your kindness and understanding that I didn't want you to go comma crazy on me. lol…..Kim Portnoy thank you so much for your friendship. I appreciate your encouragement and advice. You are destined to live out your dreams. Good luck with your project. You are my universal sister.

I like to thank **Al-Saadiq Banks** founder of **True 2 Life Productions,** my peeps and author of **No Exit, Block Party, Sincerely Yours** and **Caught 'Em Slippin'**. Al-Saadiq you have inspired me in so many ways. Thanks for making sure I linked up with the best people to help me. You are truly a stand up dude…..To my new found friend and publisher, I like to thank **Crystal Lacey Winslow** author of **Life, Love and Loneliness**, **The Criss Cross**, **Up Close and Personal** and founder of **Melodrama Publishing and Melodrama Books and Things**. You are truly a blessing. I want to thank you for giving me a chance to let the world see what I'm working with. The pen is mightier then the sword…..To my sista **Kashamba Williams** founder of **Precious Tymes,** author of **Blinded, Grimey, Driven** and **The Courts Mercy**. Thank you so much for just being you. You are an inspiration and a down chick of many talents. Thank you for the advice and your genuine kindness.

I think that about sums it up. Again I thank everyone for your help, support and faith in me. I know I forgot people, so again charge it to my head not my heart, because my heart is truly innocent.

Remember when all else fails turn to God and watch His work! I'll see y'all on the next one! Oh yeah, there will be another one!

Peace and One Love!

Endy

In Loving Memory of

Holmer Roscoe Taylor Sr.
Staci Porter
and
Floyd Bynum

CHAPTER 1

THE BEGINNING

The loud banging on the door startled Desiree "Rae-Rae" Johnson from her deep sleep. She sat up on the mattress that graced the dirty hardwood floor. Wiping the sleep from her eyes, she stood to go answer the door.

"Who the hell is it?"

"It's Roc. Bilal in there?" he shouted back.

"Y'all kill me coming over here all times of the day and night," she shouted as she opened the door.

"Rae-Rae, it's one o'clock in the afternoon. Y'all still in the bed?"

"Whatchu think?" Desiree said sarcastically, looking him up and down.

Roc stepped into the tiny one-bedroom apartment and looked around. There was paper, bottles, and cans lying on the floor. "When y'all gonna clean this shit up?"

"As much as your ass is up in here getting your head right, I don't see you offering to help clean this shit up," she spat.

"Whateva. Where's Bilal?" Roc waved her off.

Desiree stormed back into the bedroom and kicked Bilal's foot, which was resting on the floor.

"Bunchy," she shouted, calling him by his nickname. "Bunchy." She once again kicked the bottom of his foot but harder this time. He grunted and tried to lift his head. He was resting comfortably on his stomach, and he rolled over onto his back.

"What, Rae-Rae?" he shouted, irritated by the interruption.

"Roc out there for you. Get up."

He pulled his lean six-foot frame off the mattress at the speed of a turtle and stumbled dizzily as he walked out of the room with his hands shoved down the front of his dingy shorts. He had rounded shoulders and a hunched back, and his face was graced with a full, scruffy beard. He wore a tattered Afro—not by choice.

"Damn, y'all mafuckas are lazy 'round here," Roc said.

"Fuck you. Whatchu want?" Bilal asked as he plopped down onto the dirty, stained sofa laying his head back and closing his bloodshot eyes. He was sick. His legs and stomach were hurting. Before Bilal could even think about starting his day, he needed a bag to wake him up. Without his morning dose of dope, he was of no use to anyone, let alone himself.

Roc stood about six-two, weighed 240 pounds, and was solid as a rock, which was how he had gotten his name. He used to weight about 370 pounds before he ventured into the dark life of a dope fiend. Some called it P-Funk or Diesel. Back in the day he was a big baller who quickly fell victim to getting high on his own supply. He was a functioning heroin addict with no shame to his game. He enjoyed the high and the places heroin took him. Although he had chosen the life of an addict, he was still very respected by all on the streets.

Rumor had it that his hands were lethal weapons and had taken another's life a time or two. He had also acquired the reputation for being the best thief man there was—he could steal anything that wasn't cemented to the floor. With that being his now acquired hustle and heroin his drug of choice, he was feared by the streets even more.

"You want to make some money?" Roc asked, looking out of the window at the heavy activity down on the busy Fifteenth Avenue corners, one of the most drug-infested areas. Roc watched as the heroin and cocaine seekers purchased their packages then rushed off to use.

He looked over at Bilal. He knew he was sick and needed a hit to start his day. He, too, went through the same ritual every morning.

Bilal's eyes lit up; chills went through his body. Just the mere mention of money brought on the possibility of him getting his eye-awakening fix.

"Hell yeah, man. What's up?" Bilal leaned forward on the sofa.

There was a knock at the door interrupting their conversation.

"Who is it?" Bilal yelled.

"It's Tracey. Is Rae-Rae there?" the female voice asked from the other side of the door.

"Yeah, wait a minute." Bilal got up off the sofa and walked into the bedroom.

Roc walked around the living room, stepping over garbage, looking for a clean space to stand. Not having any luck, he decided to stand back in the spot in front of the window, kicking cans and bottles to the side, clearing a space. Bilal returned from the room and walked over to the door.

"She said whatchu want?" He opened the door.

Tracey was once an attractive woman. Her hair was cut short and gelled back close to her head. She wore a big green shirt, which was covered with dirty spots, and black leggings. Her eyes were hazel and her complexion light but blotchy, which came from no nutrition. Her collarbone stuck out from the lack of skin that covered her narrow body.

"Tell her I got a hit for her," Tracey said, shifting from one leg to the other like she needed to use the bathroom.

"A'ight, come in," Bilal instructed.

She walked briskly over to the sofa, stopping in her tracks when she saw Roc standing by the window.

"He's cool. Sit down. I'll get Rae-Rae for you," Bilal stated.

The woman lowered her head and sat on the sofa as she rocked back and forth looking around nervously. The anticipation for a hit was overwhelming.

"Roc man, you ain't got nothing on you now, do you?" Bilal whispered to him.

"Yeah, I got a bag that I can split with you, but it's gonna cost you a shape-up first," Roc replied.

"A'ight, hold up a minute. Let me get my clippers and tell Rae-Rae that Tracey is here for her." He disappeared into the bedroom.

Seconds later Bilal and Desiree both exited from the bedroom. Desiree motioned for Tracey to come into the kitchenette.

Bilal drug a chair over to the window where Roc stood. Roc reached into his cigarette pack and turned it upside down, shaking it. A small paper baggie fell from the box into the palm of his baseball mitt–size hands. Bilal looked at the baggie and swallowed hard. Roc began to unfold the baggie and exposed the small pile of heroin. He skillfully scooped a portion of the substance onto the pinky nail of his right finger and snorted it into his nostril. He did the same with the other nostril before passing the remaining contents to Bilal who did the same and commenced to lick the remaining residue from the baggie.

While Bilal gave Roc a haircut, Roc briefly explained to him about his plans to rob the local bowling alley. He wanted Bilal to meet the owner and show him how his plan would work.

"Hey, gurl," Tracey said as she practically ran into the kitchenette. She sat down and rocked back and forth. Desiree watched Tracey's hands shake while she retrieved the packages from her pocket.

"What's up? Whatchu got?" Desiree asked, looking desperate. Her stomach was doing flip-flops, and she felt like she had to shit.

Most free-basers felt this type of adrenaline anticipating the drug entry, causing them to get the runs, almost getting high before they actually took the hit. Once the drug entered the body, all feeling of bowel movement went away. It is said that's why a crack addict loses so much weight in a short period. The drug suppresses any desire to eat, therefore no food is entering into the body for sometimes days, but wastes leave because of the urge of the drugs' entry.

"I got two dimes," Tracey said.

She poured the contents of the two capsules onto the table. Meantime Desiree reached into the kitchen drawer, and two roaches scurried out, fleeing the light. She pulled out a rolled-up paper towel. She sat down and unraveled the paper towel, exposing two glass tubes also known as pipes or stems.

Desiree handed Tracey a stem as she passed Desiree a rock from her small pile of crack cocaine. Almost instantly the women dropped the rock at the end of the stem that contained the screens. Both women put the stem to their lips as they tilted their heads back almost at the same time. Tracey flicked her lighter as Desiree lit two matches. They touched the end of the stem containing the rock cocaine with the fire. The sizzles were heard simultaneously. The smoke bellowed its way down the stem and into their mouths, passing down into their lungs. After they took their hits, Desiree sat shaking her leg, enjoying the feeling she had from the first hit of the day as she blew the smoke from her lungs.

Tracey jumped to her feet and ran to the kitchen window while smoke escaped through her nose. She peered out of the window ducking, bobbing, and weaving as if searching for someone.

"Tray, sit yo' crazy ass down."

"Come here. Come here," Tracey yelled, waving frantically.

"What? I ain't comin' over there. Ain't nothing out there. Sit yo' ass down."

"No, for real, Rae-Rae, come here," she pleaded.

Desiree got up from her chair and walked over to the window. "What, Tray?" Desiree stood over her.

"See over there by that garbage can. Ain't that the police squattin' down over there?" Tracey said, ducking down as if not to be spotted by whomever she was hiding from.

Desiree looked by the garbage can only to see nothing but garbage.

"You know what, you a stupid bitch? You need to leave this shit alone," she yelled, walking away from the window. "See, that's why I don't be wantin' to get high wit' yo' silly ass. Every time you come over here, you pull dat same shit." She rolled her eyes.

Desiree looked over at Tracey squatting down on the floor, peeping over the top of the windowsill ledge. Desiree reached over and scooped up two more rocks, slipping one into her mouth and the other in her pipe to smoke.

Bilal went into the bedroom to change his clothes. Swatting at flies, Roc walked into the kitchenette where the women sat.

"Damn y'all be fiendin' sucking on that glass dick," he said, laughing.

"Shut up, Roc," Desiree shouted.

Tracey was still sitting underneath the windowsill on the floor and did not respond to Roc's insulting comment. She had retrieved the last rock from the table and was smoking it as she sat there paranoid and unaware that Desiree had pulled a fiend move on her. Desiree then slipped the rock from her mouth and put it into the stem and smoked it.

"Damn! Look at this bitch. Looking like a skeleton on crack." Roc continued to laugh at his own humor, pointing at Tracey crawling on the floor.

Tracey never acknowledged his presence. After taking her blast, she crawled on her hands and knees, picking up anything that resembled the crack cocaine and putting it to her tongue, tasting it.

"Tray! Get up off the floor. You ain't drop shit down there. This bitch blows my high every time," Desiree told Roc, shaking her head. "You better get up before you put some of that rat poison in your mouth that the landlord put down yesterday."

But Tracey was tweaking and wanted more crack. Her mind was playing tricks on her telling her that she dropped some.

Boom! Boom!

"What the fu—" Desiree and Roc said at the same time. Bilal ran from the room with his shirt open, jeans on, and one sneaker in his hand.

"What the hell is going on?" he announced.

Boom! Boom!

Again went the sound of something very heavy hitting against the front door. Everyone jumped. Tracey was now alert and aware of what was going on, and she stood.

"See, I told you, it's the cops," Tracey said as she twisted her lips back and forth.

"Shh! Shut up. Yo' ass is skeeted," Roc whispered.

Bilal and Roc looked at each other and approached the door together cautiously. Just as they were close to the door, it flew off its hinges, knocking Bilal to the floor. Four men ran into the apartment. The first man hit Roc with the butt end of the double-barrel shotgun he was carrying. Blood squirted everywhere, decorating the already filthy walls, adding red streaks. Roc fell to the floor like a ten-pound bag of potatoes.

Tracey began to scream.

"Shut up you, dirty bitch," another one of the gunmen yelled, aiming his Glock at her.

They all wore black hooded pullover sweatshirts with black ski masks, and all sported gloves as well.

Desiree ran to Bilal's side to try to remove the door that had fallen on top of him. Another masked gunman grabbed her by the back of her neck, squeezing hard and pulling her to her feet. Tracey continued to scream, and the rifle-toting gunman opened fire on her and blew off her right arm and half her face.

"Now if you don't want none of that, then you need to keep your anorexic ass quiet. You feel me?" the gunman said into Desiree's ear while still squeezing the back of her neck.

He appeared to be the leader, giving instructions to the others. His breath was warm and smelled of fresh violets. He threw Desiree onto the couch. Two of the gunmen lifted the door and placed it shut in the doorway. Bilal rolled over onto his side, balling into the fetal position. Desiree got down on the floor with him and held his head in her arms. The head gunman with the violet breath grabbed Roc and tried to turn him on his back.

"Damn! This mafucka is heavy as hell. Come turn his big ass over," he instructed.

The double-barrel shotgun holder stood watch over Desiree and Bilal, while the other two gunmen turned over Roc.

"Wake his ass up," the head gunman instructed.

One of the gunmen unzipped his jeans, pulled out his tool, and pissed on Roc's face.

A few seconds went by, and Roc regained his consciousness, and he began to cough. With his back turned to Bilal and Desiree, the head gunman pulled his ski mask up, exposing his face. Once Roc got a look at him, his eyes grew as big as saucers. The head gunman smiled and pulled the ski mask back over his face, and Roc began to struggle to get up. Because of Roc's size, the head gunman instructed two members to hold him down. One grabbed Roc's arms while the other held both his feet. But Roc wasn't giving up so easily, and the men struggled to hold him steady.

He pulled out a .45 that was shoved down the front of his jeans and aimed it at his forehead.

"Don't move," the head gunman grilled Roc.

Roc looked down the barrel of the big gun and laid still. The two men holding him stood, satisfied that Roc wouldn't dare try to move. Sweat poured from Roc's forehead like a leaky faucet. You could hear the whimpers from Desiree and the grunting from a hurt Bilal.

The head gunman cocked the gun and tightened his grip, but before pulling the trigger, he said. "You done robbed the wrong mafucka. See you in hell, baby."

The only thing that Desiree remembered was the loud pop and the burning smell before she blacked out.

And this was just the beginning of what went on in the hood.

CHAPTER 2

RELEASED

Desiree stepped out of the opening prison gates and into her freedom. She looked up into the sky and took a deep breath as she heard the loud clink of the prison gates closing behind her. With ninety-seven dollars, a train ticket to New Jersey, the clothes on her back, and a few items in a bag, she was free after five years serving time for accessory to armed robbery. She was sentenced to ten years and got out after five years for good behavior. Being this was her first offense with no priors, the judge was very lenient on her. He gave her five years' probation.

She boarded the prison van, taking a window seat and stared off into the distance, remembering the day Roc and Tracey had been murdered. After five years she still could see it vividly in her mind. In fact she thought about it almost every night while locked down. She really believed it was an act of God on that day. She and Bilal were supposed to be dead. She didn't know why, but the masked men walked out of the apartment and didn't harm her and Bilal.

On that terrible day in their apartment when the police investigated and questioned them, they managed to get out of being charged with the murders, which went into the police files as unsolved.

Some say they never did a thorough investigation. But why would they? It was your typical black-on-black crime over drugs. As long as one of Newark's finest wasn't being affected, there was no reason to waste man hours and paperwork over it.

Bilal and Desiree had to move from the apartment into a studio a few blocks away down the street. It didn't take long for them to get back into the swing of things and continue their lives as addicts.

Before Roc met his untimely death on that blood-curdling day, he had told Bilal the plan for the robbery that would bring them big money. Bilal decided he and Desiree would pull it off together. It was a brilliantly thought-out plan, and they were sure to come off with at least a hundred grand, if not more. Desiree agreed, and they began to execute the plan.

As she rode on the prison bus, she thought back to how she and Bilal committed the robbery that landed her in prison.

CHAPTER 3

THE PLAN

Roc was good with his hands and knew everything there was to know about electronics. He had done some work for a local bowling alley call Groovers I a few times. He was cool with the owner who use to get his cocaine from Roc back in the day, so when Roc fell off, Harry the owner helped him out by letting him come repair things when needed. Harry owned three bowling alleys—Groovers I, Groovers II, and Groovers III. Each bowling alley housed a night-club-type sports bar and restaurant in three different cities. His bowling alleys were popular and profited a lot of money.

Roc learned the routine of the money collector. They collected the money from the other bowling alleys first, making Groovers I the last stop. Roc knew that Harry would count the money in his huge office on Wednesday nights before putting it into the safe for Thursday morning's deposit. Roc was there on occasions when he had caught a glimpse of the cash all laid out on Harry's huge oak conference table in his office. His assistant fed the money into the money machine to be counted. There were no security guards in Groovers I that time of the day. The heavy-duty security came at 6:00 P.M., once everyone piled in from work. The alley and restaurant opened at 11:00 A.M. and closed at midnight during the week. The club and sports bar stayed open until 2:00 A.M. The bowling leagues usually started around 6:30 P.M.

Roc's plan was to advise Harry that he had some unfinished work to do in the office located right next to Harry's. He and Bilal planned to go there around 4:00 P.M., right after the delivery of the money, which would leave them a hour to a hour and a half tops to jack Harry and then bounce without anyone noticing.

The day of Roc and Tracey's murder, Bilal and Roc were going to the alley so that Roc could introduce him to Harry as his brother and so Bilal could get a feel of the place. So Bilal planned on going to meet with Harry to take Roc's place as his brother. He was sure that Harry would fall for it.

Bilal and Desiree arrived at Groovers I around 11:30 that Monday morning. They took baths and Bilal cut his hair. Desiree slicked her hair back with styling gel, and they then proceeded to the Salvation Army and picked out a few decent pieces of clothing.

They walked into the alley and asked the front desk clerk to speak with Harry. She advised them that he would be in at noon. They decided to sit and watch a couple bowl while they waited for Harry.

Ten minutes later, a short, fat, older-looking gentleman walked into the alley with a tall, slender beauty queen on his arm. He sported a wide-brimmed hat tilted to the side and a huge diamond pinky ring that sparkled like a disco ball.

"I bet you that's Harry," Bilal said, pointing to the gentleman.

He grabbed Desiree's hand and escorted her toward the couple. They approached the front desk where the gentleman and his companion were engaged in a conversation with the desk clerk. They all looked at Bilal and Desiree as they approached. A formal introduction was done, and they had a brief conversation about the follow-up on Roc's unfinished job. A few drinks and a couple of laughs later, Bilal and Desiree were in like Flynn.

Desiree never had any doubts that Bilal wouldn't be able to gain Harry's trust. Bilal was just that type of person. He could talk a snake into giving up his fangs. He was a charmer, and everyone who came in contact with him loved him.

For the next four weeks they learned the routines of the bowling *alley in and out, but Desiree began to grow impatient.*

"Bunchy, how long do we have to wait before we get this money? We've been casing this joint long enough."

"Listen, Rae-Rae, if you want to do something right, you have to have patience," he said, dragging on his Newport as they stood out front of the bowling alley taking a cigarette break.

"Besides the man has been paying us well. He really likes us. He may even give you a permanent job in the kitchen." Bilal flicked an ash from his cigarette. "I mean, Rae-Rae, look at us. We got a real sweet deal here, baby. We got jobs, and we get paid under the table every day at closing time. You can't beat that. Shit, we get our high on every night, and we don't have to report to work until eleven in the morning," he boasted.

"Yeah, I hear you, but hell I'm looking at that hundred G's and not having to come to work at all. Shit, yo' ass got it made. All you do is walk around all day or go up to one of them offices and go to sleep. I'm in that damn kitchen scrubbing dirty-ass pots all day," she said and rolled her eyes, flicking her cigarette butt away.

"Walk around? She-it. I be busting my ass. I don't even know about half of this electronic shit I'm doing. I know about some of it, but most of the time I'm just frontin'. Last week I got the shock of my life three times tryna get the light switch repaired. That shit went all up my damn arm," he complained as he rubbed his arm, remembering the pain he felt that day.

Desiree laughed. "Good for you...got me scrubbing dishes. Let's go because I'm telling you after this week if you're not ready to pull this off on Wednesday, I'm going to do the shit by my damn self." She walked into the building, leaving him standing outside.

CHAPTER 4

LOST

Desiree caught herself nodding off to sleep as her head dipped downward. Jerking it back up, snapping her out of her dream, she looked around to see if anyone was looking at her. As the prison van pulled up in front of the Roanoke train station, she walked past the guard sitting in the front.

"Make something of yourself, Jackson," he announced.

She didn't answer the guard. She exited the van, never to turn back. After finding a seat in the station, she waited for her 12:30 train to arrive.

She reached into her bag and pulled out a Butterfinger candy bar that was given to her by her prison cellmate Jessie. Along with the Butterfinger she had some other items that were given to her by the girls holding it down back at Roanoke Correctional Institute Facility in Virginia. As she ate her candy, she watched an attractive woman take a seat on the bench diagonally in front of her. She studied the woman from head to toe. The woman was dressed neatly in a cranberry-colored Versacé business suit. Her cranberry shoes matched to a tee. She wore her hair neatly in a wrap that fell just below her jawbone. Her makeup was light but visibly flawless. She wore a few pieces of gold jewelry that accented her cocoa skin. Desiree watched her with envy as she looked down at herself. She was wearing some government-issued jeans and a pair of Air Jordans given to her as a gift by one of the inmates.

Desiree lost her appetite and put her candy back in her bag. She looked at the schedule and saw that she had thirty minutes until the train arrived. She took the time and walked over to the ladies' room. Once inside, she approached the mirror and stared at her reflection.

"What happened to you?" she questioned herself.

Desiree stood about five-seven and had caramel smooth skin, which became healthy and smooth after going to prison and recovering from drugs. She had green eyes, which she inherited from the father she never knew.

As a child she was told her father was overseas in the Navy, but that lie didn't last long when she realized he never came home. When she became an adult, she inquired about the father that was missing from her life. Her mother told her she and a few friends had gone down to the Baltimore harbor where she met an Italian Navy man who had the most gorgeous green eyes she'd ever seen. They got drunk and had sex one time. Despite her giving him all of her contact information, she was left pregnant and never heard or saw him again.

Desiree's body had filled out since being incarcerated. She wasn't a voluptuous woman, but she had enough in the right places. She worked out while in prison with some of the other inmates, which created a solid physique with no body fat. She tucked her shirt inside her jeans then unraveled her hair from its bun, letting it fall to her shoulders. She reached in her bag for a comb and began combing her hair down.

Her soft, wavy hair was also inherited from her father. She stared at herself in the mirror, and she didn't recognize the woman who stared back at her. She had been clean for five years and never once did she realize how her life had taken a turn for the worst.

"All boarding," the conductor announced as the train came to a complete stop at the station.

The conductor stepped onto the platform, clearing the way for passengers to exit and board the train. Desiree picked up her bag, throwing it over her shoulder and boarded the train. With ticket in hand, she found a cozy seat by the window in the fourth car.

"All boarded," the conductor announced.

Soon after, the train slowly moved toward its next destination.

"Next stop, Richmond," the conductor announced over the loudspeaker.

A conductor made her way up the aisles collecting each ticket. She punched holes in the tickets and returned them to their owners. Desiree watched the chocolate-colored woman as she worked. Her haircut was very short but neatly curled. Her pointy nose seemed to lead the way as she walked. Once she arrived at Desiree, the woman gave her a pleasant smile while taking her ticket. Desiree returned the smile and retrieved her ticket from the woman. She reached into her bag and pulled out a fleece jacket, rolled it into a ball, and placed it between the window and the chair. She laid her head on it and closed her eyes. It was going to be a few hours before she reached her destination.

She thought about Bilal. The last she heard he was killed in prison two years ago. He was found hanging in his cell one morning. News traveled through the prison system on the inside almost as fast as it did on the outside. She was crushed by the news of his death. Some say that the system killed him, but it went down on record as a suicide. Desiree knew that Bilal would never take his own life. Now he was gone forever, and she didn't know what she was going to do out on the streets alone.

They use to write each other, but they had lost contact when he was transferred to upstate New York. Bilal had life with no possibility of parole for murder and armed robbery. She missed him so much. He was her heart, her soul mate, her everything. Now she would have to face the world on her own. She would always tell him, if it weren't for her greediness, they would have never gotten caught. Through the letters they wrote each other, he was constantly giving her hope to make it through one day at a time.

She cried a silent cry for her man. She loved him so much and didn't know if she would be able to go on living without him. While thinking of Bilal, she drifted off into a deep sleep.

CHAPTER 5

BACKPEDALING

"Newark Penn Station," the conductor announced over the train's PA system.

Desiree opened her eyes and stretched her arms. She had slept the whole ride back to Newark. She gathered her things and exited the train into the muggy air. The train's fumes mixed with humidity were suffocating. She merged in with the train's crowd and left the platform. The escalator wasn't working so she had to walk down the heavy steel steps. Once in the station, she looked around at all the people hustling to their destinations. She walked past the various newsstands and eateries. The aroma of food and bad air filled her nostrils.

Home sweet home, she said to herself.

She walked past a hotdog stand. "I ain't had one of them in years," she said aloud.

She purchased a foot-long hotdog and a Pepsi. She gobbled down the hotdog and sipped on her soda as she walked through the station, taking in the scenery. Once outside, lines and lines of taxicabs hugged the curb. Rows of cars pulled up and away after either dropping off or picking up passengers. She didn't know which way to go. She had no destination. She had been dreading this day although she longed for her freedom. Without Bilal she didn't know where to begin again. What family she had left had disowned her. The friends she had before she started using were afraid of her, so the only people she knew as family were the addicts with whom she had surrounded herself.

People, places, and things, she thought. *I cannot associate myself with people, places, and things of my drug-used past.*

She didn't know what to do. She came back to Newark because that's where she was from. She didn't have enough money to stay in a motel. She needed a place to stay and food to eat. As she leaned against a wall, it hit her. She would visit an old friend of hers who didn't use. Unfortunately she would have to go back to the old neighborhood, but what other choice did she have?

She went into her bag, pulled out her pack of cigarettes, and lit one. As she smoked it a derelict man walked up to her.

"You got one you can spare, miss?" he asked in his inebriated state.

His odor lit the hairs in her nose. She reached into her pack and gave the man a cigarette.

"Thank you, ma'am. Got a light?" he asked, holding the cigarette between his filthy fingers.

Desiree lit the man's cigarette with her matches and shook the fire out, throwing the dead match to the ground.

"Thank you, ma'am. Do you have any change you can spare to get me something to eat?" the man asked.

She reached into her pocket and gave him the few coins she had. She walked away from the homeless man, thinking back on how she used to beg for spare change just to get high.

She headed toward a cab. She opened the door and got in.

"Where to lady?" the driver asked.

"Fifteenth Avenue." She leaned her head back and closed her eyes. *What the hell am I doing? Where else am I supposed to go? I just gotta be strong. I gotta stay strong. God, give me strength.*

ON THE OTHER SIDE OF TOWN

"Yo, son, you musta forgot who I am. I'm dat nigga. You heard me?" a young boy named Rich boasted.

"Man, that's bullshit. Ain't no way in hell you twisted that niggaz spleen. You full of shit man," a kid named Dale proclaimed.

"Word up, man. I'm tryna tell you. I bodied dat nigga and left his ass leaking," Rich continued to brag.

"Y'all on a break?" a deep voice boomed from behind.

The two boys jumped and turned around.

"Oh, what's up, Ish? Naw, man, we was just shootin' the shit," Rich stuttered.

"I don't pay y'all mafuckas to shoot the shit. Is my paper right? Y'all outta work? What's up?" he continued to question.

"Naw, man, we still got work," Rich stammered.

"Explain something to me. Y'all tryna tell me y'all still got work, y'all ain't got my ends ready, and y'all standing around holding ya dicks? Am I missing something?" Ishmael asked, folding his arms across his well-proportioned chest.

Technically Ishmael was *dat nigga*. He was caked up and well respected in the streets and getting money in South Carolina, D.C., and Virginia.

The boys looked at each other with their mouths hanging open, trying to think of something to say. Ishmael shook his head at the boys in disappointment. He reached into his pocket. The boys backed up out of fear. Everybody knew that Ishmael always carried a hammer.

"I'm not feeling this situation right now. I'm feeling violated," Ishmael stated as he popped a piece of violet candy in his mouth that he had retrieved from his pocket.

"Naw, Ish man, it ain't like that," Rich said.

"Rich, you'll never make lieutenant, let alone be one of my top soldiers at the rate you're going." He narrowed his eyes, and a frown came across his face. "Y'all mafuckas get back on your post. And my grip better be right," he said, growling.

The boys took off running like scared rabbits, holding up their sagging jeans.

Ishmael looked back at his boy Derrick approaching and shook his head.

"Rik man, I don't know what's up with these knuckleheads. I need me some real soldiers," Ishmael told his friend.

"Yeah, like the old squad we had back in the day," Derrick agreed.

"Yeah, man, and the fucked-up thing about it is these little mafuckas constantly try me at all times. I see I'm gonna have to make an example outta one of them hard-headed niggaz to send a message to the rest."

Derrick nodded in agreement and kept sucking on the toothpick that protruded from the corner of his mouth.

The two men continued to watch over the strip to make sure everything was on point. Most men in Ishmael's position would send their lieutenants out to check on things, but not Ishmael. He was always on the grind, checking up on his blocks personally. He never wanted to be that type of cat who sent messages; he wanted his runners to know that he was still very much in the game. In fact, he and Derrick had just arrived back in town. They had been gone for two weeks from checking up on his territories in other states. He felt that hugging the blocks would boost workers' morale and insure that business would be on point. His hands never got dirty by handling the product, but trust and believe he was there to make sure his grip was right.

Back in the day, Ishmael and Derrick terrorized the town. Not that they weren't still feared, but over the years, they had matured and were more educated in the game. Back then they were wild gun-busting, didn't-give-a-fuck type dudes who were on the come-up and did whatever it took to get money.

Ishmael had a squad of real soldiers behind him then. Their loyalty was unbelievable. Most of his soldiers would take a bullet for him like they were secret service men and he was the president. He treated them well and kept their pockets fat. Everybody who was linked to Ishmael ate well. But those times were gone. Most of his loyal soldiers were either dead or doing crazy numbers in prison. Ishmael kept their commentary laced for those who were locked up.

The two men stopped in front of the local bodega.

"Rik man, go cop me some more candy and a Black and Mild."

Derrick nodded, twirled the toothpick in his mouth, and disappeared into the store. Ishmael leaned up against the building and continued to survey the area.

Ishmael was thirty years old, and he stood six-two. His body was built like a running back. His complexion was dark and smooth. He had a thin mustache and long, thin sideburns that connected to his thin-shaved beard. He had shoulder-length zig-zag-designed cornrows all going to the back. He was laced with an iced-out necklace with a cross medallion covered with tiny diamonds. His attire was thuggish but stylishly neat. He was a lady's chocolate dream.

Ishmael saw one of his loyal workers approaching.

"What's up, Ish?"

"What's good, D?" Ishmael said to one of his last committed soldiers whose name was Damon.

The two men shook hands and bumped shoulders.

"It's all good, baby."

"That's what's up." Ishmael nodded. "You heard anything from that kid Rallo?"

"Naw, man. The crew still out looking for him."

"Get the word out that as soon as he's located that I want him brought directly to me."

"Yo, Ish, let me push that nigga's wig back," Damon said eagerly.

"Easy, D. Never let your emotions get the best of you. I schooled you about that before."

"Yeah, I know, Ish, but—"

"But nothing," Ishmael interrupted. "You wanna hand in your stripes? So what, you wanna be a part of security now?"

"Naw, Ish, it ain't dat," he said, lowering his head.

"Listen, D, you the last of the best clique I ever had. You know the game. Slow your roll. You the student and I'm the teacher. You feel me?"

"No doubt, Ish. I feel you. Good looking."

"You straight?"

"I'm good, Ish," Damon said as he gave Ishmael dap and moved on.

Derrick returned from the store and handed Ishmael his requested purchase. A hunter-green Cadillac hugged the curb as it turned onto the avenue. It came to a full stop in front of the bodega where Ishmael and Derrick stood. The back window lowered, and Ishmael approached the car.

"OG, what's good?" Ishmael asked with a wide grin.

"Ain't nothing, youngblood, I'm just struggling and striving, tryna survive. Whatchu know good?" The husky voice filtered from the backseat of the car.

"You, OG. I'm tryna get where you at," Ishmael stated.

A hearty laugh boomed from the car.

"Get in, youngun. I want to rap with you for a minute."

Ishmael gave Derrick the sign to look out for him until he got back. Derrick nodded and twirled his toothpick.

Derrick was about the same height as Ishmael. He was much bigger than Ishmael was in size—whereas Ishmael was the running back, Derrick was built like a line backer. He sported long dreads, which he kept tied in a knot in the back of his head. He had brown skin and bore a striking resemblance to actor Duane Martin. He kept his face shaved clean. He liked it like that because no one knew his real age. He looked to be about twenty-three but in actuality he was thirty-five.

Derrick seemed to be the quiet type. He always looked like he was in deep thought, contemplating things. His body size and humility created the illusion of him being a gentle giant, but in reality Derrick was any human being's worst nightmare. His low, quiet demeanor and captivating vibe caused people to underestimate him, and that very same thing had cost many victims their lives.

He wasn't always Ishmael's right-hand man. He use to have his own crew called the Mob Squad. They weren't stickup kids, but they were enforcers. They were paid by different organizations to go collect debts, security, and clean-up crew. If you wanted someone to disappear then the Mob Squad was the crew to do the job. If there was a body to get rid of, they came and cleaned up the mess, leaving no traces.

Derrick and Ishmael hooked up when they met in the county when Ishmael was booked on a drug charge and Derrick caught a gun charge. The two hit it off instantly, and the rest was history. They'd been friends for more than twelve years. They had a tight bond. Ishmael was the only person who understood Derrick's demeanor and his strange ways.

Ishmael climbed into the car and settled into the soft, plush seats. The hog pulled away from the curb like a graceful ballerina.

"So you still hanging out on the corners, huh, youngblood?"

"Well, you know how that goes…I gotta keep my eye on my operation."

"What I tell you about that, son? That's what you got lieutenants for."

Ishmael sat in thought as the smooth sounds of Marvin Gaye crooned from the car's speakers.

"Leroy, I was thinking about what you told me the other day…"

"Yeah?"

"Yeah, I think I'm gonna pass on that, man. I got my own thing going, and I like the way it's flowing. I been in this game for a long time."

"You said it right there, youngblood," Leroy said. "You been in this business a long time, and you still doing the same ole shit. You can't be out there in the mix of things. That's how you catch them big figures doing time in the joint. You need to come on board. How do you think that I've manage to stay out of the joint all these years?"

"I don't know. I never really gave it any thought," Ishmael responded.

"Because I was smart. I used my head."

"I feel you, Leroy, but I ain't for all that politic shit. I'm from the hood, and that's where I'm comfortable."

"I'm from the hood, too, nigga. You think I was born rich? No, I had to get mine the hard way. But with politics the way they are, you ain't gonna last long in this business, son."

"Leroy man, I know what I'm doing. When they bring the heat and rolled up on me, they never have nothing to stick on me," Ishmael reasoned.

"Yeah, youngblood, but you're not listening. They want you bad. You don't think they know what you're doing, son? They know every move you make. All they got to do is get one of them little punks you got running for you to talk, and it's all over for you, son."

"Naw, man, my peoples are loyal," Ishmael assured.

"Shit," Leroy said, laughing, "these little sperm donors out here don't know shit about being loyal. Have I ever steered you wrong?"

"Naw."

"Well then hear me out. I can help you. I know a lot of people downtown. They can protect you. They can make it easy for you to keep your empire going."

"Yeah, but what I gotta do to get that?" Ishmael asked.

"Shit, youngblood, ain't nothing for free in this world," Leroy said, lighting a Cuban cigar.

Ishmael stared at the cigar as it protruded from Leroy's mouth, looking like a huge tree trunk. The pinky ring he sported glistened, almost blinding him.

Leroy was one of the big doggs. He was an original gangster with more than forty years in the game. He was well groomed and didn't look a day over forty, although he was sixty-two. He owned most of the car washes, Laundromats, and Super food stores and had real estate all over the tri-states. He still had his hands in the drug game as one of the top suppliers, but for the most part, most of his businesses were legit.

"What you getting outta the deal?" Ishmael asked, breaking the silence.

Leroy laughed and continued to puff on the cigar. Huge clouds of smoke filled the air. Leroy cracked the window, and the smoke bellowed its way out into the night air.

"Well, the kind of protection I'm gonna be giving you is worth some compensation. I gotta grease palms to get you that protection, so naturally my palm will need some greasing," he said, looking over at Ishmael.

Ishmael looked out the window as the hog cruised the streets. He liked the smooth ride of the car. He wasn't a Caddy man, but he liked the way it felt.

"So what do you say?" Leroy asked.

"I'll let you know. Let me think on it some more."

"Your dime and your time, youngun. Don't be so stupid that you can't see the forest for the trees."

Ishmael looked at Leroy, confused. Leroy bellowed out yet another hearty laugh. "Think about it and get back to me."

"A'ight."

The Caddy pulled up to the curb just two blocks from where it had picked up Ishmael. He got out of the car and watched the car trail down the street. Ishmael started the walk toward the corner where he left his friend Derrick standing.

"So what was that about?" Derrick asked, handing him the Black and Mild.

"About that shit I told you about before with them downtown mafuckas."

"Man, fuck that shit. We ain't rolling over so those mafuckas can stick us in the ass," Derrick retorted.

"Word," Ishmael stated as he began to shamp the Black and Mild.

"Yo, anybody ever tell you that you look a little just like that mafucka Leroy?"

"Yeah, man, all my life," Ishmael said, popping a match, lighting the cigar.

CHAPTER 6

Old Friend

Back across town

"Okay, lady, this is your stop," the taxi cab driver announced.

Desiree looked around the old neighborhood. Everything basically looked the same. A lot of new faces flocked the block, but it was still the same traffic flow.

"You gonna get out?" the cabdriver asked.

"Um...yeah."

She went into her pocket and paid the cabby. She reluctantly opened the door and stepped out. The cab pulled away from the curb. Desiree stood on the sidewalk and looked around as if she was a stranger to the neighborhood. She looked in everyone's face that walked past her. She tried to see if there was anyone she recognized. Desiree found herself standing in front of the building where she and Bilal used to live, and a chill ran over her entire body. The place was abandoned and boarded up. She wanted to cry as she relived the past standing right there on the streets.

"Red tops! Got them red tops," a man yelled.

"What up, ma? Got them red tops. You need anything?" he asked her.

"I'm good," she said, shaking her head at the man as she viewed the contents in his hand.

Desiree found herself walking the streets in search of her friend. She had gone by where her friend used to live, only to be disappointed that she had since moved.

As she walked, she spotted the old friend she had been looking for coming out of the liquor store. Beverly wasn't an addict, but she was an alcoholic. She used to come up to Desiree's apartment with her boyfriend who used both heroin and cocaine. Some call it speed balling.

Desiree, Bilal, and Beverly's boyfriend, Mike, would get high, and Beverly would drink her liquor. She had two kids and an apartment on the same block. Beverly was a good woman, and Desiree loved her company.

"Bev," she called out to her.

Beverly turned around.

"Rae-Rae?" She squinted.

"Yeah, it's me."

"Get the hell outta here. What's up, girl?" Beverly shouted, walking toward her.

The two women embraced. Desiree could smell the foul, stale alcohol odor coming from her. They stood back and looked at each other. Beverly exposed a rotten-tooth smile.

"Damn, girl. You look good. When you get out?"

"I just came home."

"Where you headed?" Beverly asked.

"That's what I'm tryna figure out. I don't know where to go," Desiree stated sincerely.

"I feel you, girl." She suddenly looked down at her feet. "How you taking Bunchy's death?"

"You know about that?" she asked, surprised.

"Hell yeah. Now since when you known me not to know the low down on anything that goes on in the hood?"

"You right, but he died in a prison upstate, not in the hood."

"I got ways of finding things out," she boasted.

There was an awkward silence between the two women as they walked. Desiree felt the tears welling up in her eyes.

"It sure is good to see you. I missed you, girl," Beverly said, putting her arm around Desiree's shoulder, trying to change the subject.

"You still with Mike?" she inquired as she wiped the tears from her eyes.

"Please. Mike got locked up."

"For real?"

"Yep. A lot of things have changed around here."

"I can tell. There are a lot of new faces out here. A lot of young boys, too," Desiree said, looking around.

Beverly dug into her brown paper bag and unscrewed the top to her bottle of poison. She peeled the bag back, and Desiree watched her turn the bottle up to her chapped lips and take a deep gulp of the poison.

"Yeah, a lot of people you use to run with are gone, girl," she said, screwing the top back onto the bottle.

"Gone? Gone where?"

"Dead or in jail. Hey, Cookie went to rehab and got clean. I heard she's doing real good. She moved down south too."

"Wow, that's good."

The two women continued to walk down the street.

"Hey, Rae-Rae, if you want, you can stay with me."

"I don't know, Bev…you got kids, and I don't want to get in the way."

"Get in the way of what? Please, girl, you can stay with me. You know you my girl." She smiled.

"I don't have much money. I'm going to go and join this program my counselor told me about. I've been out of work for a long time. Did you know I had marketing skills as a top buyer?"

"Yeah," Beverly drawled, "I remembered you told me before."

"So I'm tryna get back into that. After I finish the program, they're supposed to send me to school to improve my skills, then I'm gonna get me a good job. I gotta get my life back on track."

"I hear you, girl. I can't go to nobody's school though. School wasn't never for me. Nope, I'm gonna keep doing what I'm doing and enjoy myself," Beverly stated proudly.

Beverly was a master at robbing the system. She received three hundred dollars a month in food stamps and got five hundred dollars a month welfare for two kids—eleven-year-old Tony Jr. and nine-year-old Michaela.

She paid a hundred dollars a month for rent, and she received energy checks to pay her utilities. Beverly milked the system for all that it's worth.

She got furniture vouchers every two years and appliance vouchers every three years. She sold the vouchers to locals or whoever would buy them.

The attractive days were long gone for Beverly. She had missing teeth, and the ones she still had were rotting. She had beautiful wavy hair that she kept in a ponytail. She stood five-two and had a brown liver-spotted complexion.

Everyone knew her, and she knew everyone and their business as well. Beverly was the 411 of the hood. If she didn't know it, she would surely find it out for you.

"I went by your old place and found out that you moved. Where did you move to?" Desiree asked as the two continued to walk.

"I'm on Eighteenth Avenue now. I got me a two-bedroom, and it's got a service porch that I can use as a bedroom. You can have that if you want, and I can get you a bed."

"That's cool. I'm not going to be there long anyway," she said.

But in the back of Desiree's mind, it wasn't cool. She just hoped that Eighteenth Avenue wasn't anything like it was when she left with drugs, addicts, and more drugs cluttering the corners. Desiree just prayed that she would be able to maintain her sobriety.

CHAPTER 7

CAN NOT LET GO

Two days had past, and Desiree was sitting in her room at Beverly's apartment. It was a quaint apartment on the second floor in a four-family duplex that sat in the middle of the block. It was clean and decorated with the new furniture that Beverly acquired from the state. She didn't have any pictures hanging on the walls, but nonetheless the apartment was comfortable. The downfall to living with Beverly was the noisy neighbors and drug trafficking that went on down below on the street corners.

It was the first of the month, and Desiree was watching the news in her room while Beverly waited downstairs on the street for the mailman to bring her welfare check and food stamps.

The mailman came, and Beverly went to the liquor store to cash her check. When Beverly returned, she asked Desiree to go with her to the grocery store. Desiree didn't want to go, but she figured she would have to leave the apartment sooner or later. She said a prayer and was off to the Super food store to shop.

To her surprise Beverly took her clothes shopping as well. She only bought her a few things, but Desiree was happy just being able to put the government-issued jeans away for a few days.

They arrived home and put away the food, and Beverly prepared dinner. It was only 3:30 in the afternoon, but she couldn't wait to eat. She hadn't had a home-cooked meal in a long time. Since she'd been living with Beverly she'd only eaten sandwiches made by the corner store that Beverly went and got for her. She was down to thirty dollars from her commissary money.

The new bed Beverly had gotten her was a twin. It was small but better then the cot she slept on in the facility.

Desiree sat on her bed after eating dinner. She was full and satisfied.

"Hey, Rae-Rae, you want to come out on the block with me?"

Desiree shook her head without looking her way, continuing to stare at the television.

Beverly sat down on the bed next to her. "What's wrong, Rae-Rae?"

"I don't want to be around that shit, Bev. If I'm gonna stay clean, I gotta stay clear."

"I feel you, but you don't have to be around it. I'm just gonna sit on the porch and get some air. That's all. Plus, they be on the corner, not in front of the house."

She was sincere but Desiree was afraid.

"I know, Bev, but you don't understand."

Both women sat in silence.

"Is it because of Bunchy dying?" Beverly asked.

Desiree didn't say a word, looking down at her fingers instead. Finally she spoke. "That's not the only thing, Bev. I mean my life is a mess. All I do is have nightmares, about the murders too."

That was the first time either one of them had mentioned that horrible day.

"You know they never found out who did it, Bev."

"I know."

"But what bothers me the most is I went and did some ole greedy shit to get me and Bunchy locked up, with him doing life. And then the bullshit came when they said he killed himself. Killed himself, Bev? No way in hell would he do that. I don't know what I'm gonna do, Bev." She placed her hands over her face. "Bunchy was all I had. He taught me everything I knew about the streets. I knew nothing about this game when I met him. I miss him so much. I'm so scared to be out here by myself," she cried.

"I know how you feel, Rae-Rae," she said, patting her on the shoulder. "But you a big girl. You said it yourself, Bunchy taught you everything you know about the streets. You a survivor, girl. You can do it."

"I can't do it without Bunchy."

"Rae-Rae, listen, girl, you can't depend on no man to make you complete. Them mafuckas will bring you down, girl. You was a successful businesswoman before you met Bunchy, and look what happened. You depended on him to make you complete, and he wound up getting you hooked on drugs."

Desiree looked at her as if she had some nerve talking.

"I know I'm an alcoholic," Beverly said, noticing the look, "but ain't no man make me this way. This was my choice, and I ain't wanting for nothing. My kids are fed and clothed. My place is nice. I gets paid and the whole nine. But dis ain't about me, Rae-Rae. It's about you. I ain't scared to go outside. You is."

With that, Beverly got up and left the house. Desiree sat staring off into space. She knew it wasn't Beverly's fault she felt the way she did. She also knew Beverly was right. She used to be a strong black woman. She supervised the toughest of men and dominated with an iron fist. All she wanted to do was go to sleep. If she went to sleep, she wouldn't have to think about it. This is something she became accustomed to doing while being incarcerated. In the beginning she slept a lot so as not to think about the horrible murders—until recently the nightmares came.

CHAPTER 8

TRUST ISSUE

It was 7:00 A.M. and the phone was ringing. Ishmael rolled over and grabbed the phone.

"Yeah."

"Ish man, we got that package," Derrick said.

"A'ight. Where?" he whispered.

"I'm on the way to pick it up. I'll meet you at the spot."

"Get at me when you get there," Ishmael croaked.

He hung up the phone and rested his arm across his forehead. The lovely lady who lay next to him threw her arm across his chest. He reached down, grabbing her arm, and he began to plant soft kisses up it. She giggled. He reached her lips and kissed her deeply.

"What you getting into today?" he asked.

"I'm gonna do some shopping."

"That's all you do."

"Oh, that reminds me. I need some money," she said.

"I just gave you a stack day before yesterday."

"I know but I had to use it. I had to pay some bills, and then there was this outfit I had to have. I want to go and pick that up today," she whined.

"Damn, baby, you spending the money faster than I can make it."

"Oh, stop your complaining. You got more money than you can

handle," she retorted.

Ishmael got out of bed and headed toward the bathroom. He stood in front of the mirror and prepared to brush his teeth.

The woman who lay in his bed was his on- and off-again girlfriend, Zola. She was Jamaican and was brought over to the United States when she was five. She didn't have an accent but she was fluent in her native language.

They just had gotten back together three weeks ago. Derrick always tried to tell Ishmael about Zola. He referred to her as a "gold-digging bitch." Ishmael had one weakness, and that was Zola. He loved her deeply. No matter how many times he'd busted her with other dudes, he'd always take her back after she'd sex him crazy.

Zola was good at her game. She was straight from the street—a diva at heart. She knew what ballers were holding paper, and she knew what to do to get at that paper. She was a master at her skills. She pimped Ishmael on a regular. She did care about him, but it could go either way. It wasn't like she was in love with him. If he weren't in the picture, she wouldn't lose sleep over it. She would move on to the next baller. For the moment, she had a good thing going, and she was not about to lose it. She also knew how far to push him. Every man had his limit. Even though Ishmael was sweet on Zola, he was still one of the most notorious gangster dealers out there.

He never mixed business with pleasure, and he knew how to separate his feelings for Zola from his business. Each time he caught Zola out there creeping with another square, he handled himself in leadership manner, but was ruthless enough so as to set an example for all who watched him.

One time, Ishmael, Derrick, a few of his crew and security men went out one Saturday night. They had just pulled up in front of a club where a heroin baller named Duke was giving a party.

They walked up into the club like they owned it. Everybody knew who Ishmael and his crew were, and they gave them much respect. Once inside they were directed straight to the VIP room upstairs, which overlooked the entire club. You could do anything in this VIP room, and mostly anyone in there, did. Little Cash, a member of the crew, pulled out the blunts, and the men smoked, drank Cristal, and watched the scene.

An hour had passed when Derrick tapped Ishmael and directed his attention to the center of the dance floor. There in the middle was Zola dancing with some low-count dealer from another town named Lo-Lo. The way Zola was grinding Lo-Lo, it looked like he'd bust a nut right in his pants. They where dancing to Sean Paul featuring Sasha "I'm Still in Love with You."

She was wearing a tight leather coochie skirt that inched up higher and higher every time she rolled her ass. The dude was humping on Zola so hard, that every man watching had to have gotten a hard-on.

Ishmael looked over at his boys as they were looking at him waiting to see how he was going to handle the situation. Ishmael knew he had to do something, and it had to be something of leadership action to spare himself the embarrassment.

He tried to act as if it didn't bother him as rage began to fill his body. He got up from his seat and high-tailed it downstairs with his boys in tow.

Once he reached the dance floor, he stood and observed with the veins protruding from his neck. He clenched his jawbone, and he approached the couple. Ishmael snatched Zola up by the arm.

"What are you doing, Ishmael?" she screamed, holding her arm.

"No, what the fuck are you doing?" He was calm. "Take yo' ass home." He shoved her.

"You know this clown?" Lo-Lo said, pointing at Ishmael.

"Yo, fam, that really ain't none of your bizness. Let's go, Zola," he demanded.

"Yo, wait. Hold the fuck up. Who is you?" Lo-Lo directed his question to Ishmael.

"Like I said fam, this ain't got nothing to do witchu," Ishmael warned.

"Yo, mafucka." Lo-Lo pushed Ishmael in the chest, not budging him an inch.

Ishmael stepped forward, and before Lo-Lo could blink, Ishmael had landed a right hook to his jaw. Stunned, Lo-Lo stumbled backward, holding his jaw.

Lo-Lo reached for his burner, but before he could whip it out, Derrick was up on him with a quickness with his nine-millimeter jabbed into Lo-Lo's stomach.

"Yo, nigga, let me introduce you to the belly of the beast," Derrick said, his fiery eyes warning him.

Lo-Lo dropped his shoulders and looked around to see the squad had him surrounded. He knew he was outnumbered.

"Punk ass," Lo-Lo mouthed, looking at Ishmael.

Ishmael smirked with confidence.

"We got a problem over here," Duke yelled as he stepped into the middle of the altercation with his squad behind him.

"Naw, fam, no problem—" Ishmael looked back at Lo-Lo—"right?"

"Oh, a'ight 'cause if this nigga poppin' off, Ish man, I could take care of this punk proper like for ya," Duke projected over the loud music.

"Naw, Duke, I'm good. Good lookin' though," Ishmael assured him. "Yo, Rik man, we out," Ishmael shouted.

He grabbed Zola by the hand and floated toward the exit. Once outside they all descended to their vehicles. He mushed Zola in her head, never saying a word to her as they walked. Although she knew he was pissed, she knew better then to say anything at that moment. She knew that she was wrong, and she wasn't a fool either. He was heated and would do anything to show off in front of his friends. He had told her time and time again not to show her ass in front of his boys.

That situation just like many others ended their relationship, but then weeks later they got back together.

Ishmael came back to the present and finished grooming himself and entered into the bedroom. He walked into his walk-in closet, which took up almost the entire wall. He had rows and rows of fitted caps, sneakers, shoes, and boots. He had every name-brand pair of jeans lining the other side of the wall. He had all his designer sweaters and suits on one portion of the back wall, and his jerseys and button-up shirts lined the other half of the back wall. He turned on the light and prepared to select his gear for the day.

He heard Zola's cell phone ring. Zola walked past the closet and headed for the bathroom all the while whispering on her cell phone. Ishmael wondered why all the whispering. He went to the bathroom door and listened. He couldn't hear much, but it appeared she was talking to a dude.

Ishmael burst into the bathroom, breaking the doorjamb. Zola jumped up from the toilet. She closed her cell phone and peered at him.

"Who was that on the phone?" he asked as his nose flared.

"Why, Ishmael? Don't start tripping."

"Who the fuck was that on the phone?"

"Why?"

"Because I asked you, Zo." He remained calm.

"It was my modda, Ishmael."

"Your mother, huh? You think I'm stupid?"

"I don't know what you are, but I do know you're tripping right now." She rolled her eyes.

Zola tried to walk out of the bathroom, but he stopped her by pushing her backward. "Come on, Ishmael, let me out."

"Who was that nigga you was on the phone with?" he asked as calm as he could be.

"I wasn't on the phone with no nigga. Just leave me alone," she shouted.

"A'ight. So it's like that?"

"Yeah, it's like that."

"I swear, Zola, if I find out you fucking around with another nigga, we finished," he said, leaving the bathroom.

"Whatever, Ishmael. Ain't nobody doing nothing."

His mind was racing. He no longer trusted her. He knew something was going on. He was so tired of the games she played. He always thought the saying, you can't turn a whore into a housewife was bullshit. When he met Zola, he didn't consider her a whore, even though rumor said it. He always thought she was too sophisticated to stoop to that level. But the more he thought about it, deep down in his gut, he was starting to believe it.

He pushed the thought out of his mind and continued to dress. Minutes later, Zola came into the room stark naked. He looked up at her. Her skin was flawlessly smooth. There wasn't a single spot on it. It was black as night, and it glowed. Her ass looked like two basketballs mounted on her lower back. Her breasts favored two grapefruits sitting up on her chest.

Zola knew what she was doing. She knew Ishmael couldn't resist her beauty. She had taken a shower. She walked over to the dresser drawer and bent over to retrieve a pair of panties from the bottom drawer. Ishmael felt himself rising. He tried to fight the urge off by turning away from her. He continued to put on his sneakers and lace them.

She then walked past him to get to the other side of the room, throwing her ass hard as she walked. She hadn't put on her panties yet. She bent over again in front of him, pretending to be searching for something in the basket of clothes that sat on the floor. He looked at her pussy, which was exposed to him. His tool stiffened, and fighting the urge was no longer an option.

Ishmael stood and made his way over to her. He unzipped his jeans, letting them drop to the floor. He pulled down his boxer shorts and grabbed his tool. As Zola bent over, he entered her, and an explosion went off in his head. The feeling was so overwhelming, he didn't know if he would be able to hold on without releasing too soon. Zola threw her grind on him like a true Jamaican woman. If she continued to stroke him the way she did, Ishmael knew he wouldn't be able to hold on. Minutes later, he pulled out and dumped cum on her backside.

After cleaning himself, he walked out of the bathroom to his ringing cell phone. It was Derrick telling him that he had made it to the spot with the package.

Ishmael looked at Zola as she began to dress. He felt a certain distance from her. He didn't understand it, but he knew one thing. He didn't trust her—even though the sex was off the hook.

"You gonna give me the money or not, Ishmael?" she asked with a little more attitude than he cared to hear.

"No. Get whoever you were talking to on the phone to give it to you. Oh yeah, that was your mother, right? Well ask her for the money." Ishmael walked out of the room.

Zola was heated. She waited until Ishmael left the house and went into the back of his closet and pulled the small lever that loosened a portion of the wall. She then removed the panel. Behind the wall was a compartment that held a safe and a shelf. She didn't know the combination to the safe, but Ishmael kept small piles of money on the shelf for easy access. She grabbed a small stack of money and put the panel back. Zola left the house, heading for the mall.

CHAPTER 9

THE PACKAGE

Ishmael pulled up in front of a tattered two-family house also known as their stash house. The house needed a paint job badly. The brick steps leading to the porch had seen better days. They were broken and some were missing. He walked through the front doors of the house and down the hall of the first floor. He searched for the key on his key ring and entered into the apartment. There were a few pieces of furniture sprawled around the front room. He walked through the kitchen into the rear room. Derrick and three of the crewman were waiting for his arrival.

The package was tied to a chair. His name was Rallo. He looked to be twenty years old. He had been beaten. One side of his face was swollen from the punishment he was given. Dried blood covered his lips. A sock was shoved into his mouth. His eyes widened when Ishmael appeared in the room. Rallo began to squirm and try to speak. One of the men slapped him across the face with the back of his hand. Rallo's head snapped back from the force of the blow. His breathing became short and hard.

"What up, Rallo?" Ishmael asked.

Rallo began to mumble.

"Take that sock out of his mouth," Ishmael instructed no one in particular.

The sock was removed. Ishmael grabbed one of the chairs that sat in the room and placed it directly in front of Rallo.

"Ish man, what's up with this, man?"

"Where you been?" he said, sitting down on the chair backward.

"My grandmother got sick so I had to go down south with my moms to help out," Rallo stated, looking as serious as he could.

"Oh yeah? So how your grandmoms doing now?" Ishmael asked as if he really cared.

"She a'ight now."

"A'ight. I'm glad to hear that. So where's my money?" Ishmael stated, looking Rallo dead in his eyes.

Rallo fidgeted as he tried to keep eye contact. "What money you talking about, Ish?"

"My fuckin' five thousand dollars," Ishmael said, remaining calm.

Ishmael stood. "Before you answer my question, just know that your answer decides whether you keep breathing."

"Ish, I don't have no money that belongs to you, I swear," Rallo pleaded.

Ishmael shook his head. "Wrong answer, Rallo." He folded his arms across his chest, revealing the strength of his muscular arms. "As a matter of fact, I know you took my money. You want to know how I know you took it?" Not waiting for an answer, he continued, "Because you the only nigga in town who's got a tattoo of a snake going around your neck. When you and your stickup punks robbed one of my men, he saw the tat. Although you had on a ski mask your neck was exposed." He was silent for a few seconds and spoke again. "I'm gonna ask you again and keep it funky. Where is my fuckin' money?" he stated calmly.

"Ish, I would never disrespect you like dat. I respect you. I been tryna get on your payroll for a minute now. That's why I hung around your crew so that they could tell you about me. I wanted to show you my loyalty," Rallo cried. Tears streamed down his face, and his words were barely audible.

"Get on my payroll, huh?" Ishmael gave an evil laugh, sounding like the Jackal. "Maybe you hung around my squad to set me up. You ain't nothing but a nickel-and-dime nigga anyway."

"Ish, I didn't rob you, man. That's what I'm tryna tell you," he pleaded.

"A'ight, check this out. Give me the names of the two dudes who was with you who robbed my boy, and I'll let you go."

Rallo tried to speak, but Ishmael threw up his hand to silence him.

"Let's just say the third person wasn't you. In fact I don't even want to know who the third person was. Just tell me who the other two were."

Ishmael walked over to the window and looked out into the backyard. Garbage was all over the yard. Old furniture lined the fence. Two old mattresses were placed in the middle of the yard by the neighborhood's youth. They would do somersaults on the mattresses when playing.

Rallo tried to turn his head to follow Ishmael. "I don't know who they were, Ish."

"So you would rather kick my back in than to tell me who took my money?" he said, still looking out the window.

"No, man, I ain't kick'n yo' back in," Rallo cried.

"So who got my money?"

"I heard it was Donald and Ronald," he said, coughing.

Ronald and Donald where identical twin brothers. They where two-bit hustlers who did nothing but rob niggaz to get money.

"Oh, Ron and Don got my money?" Ishmael turned and looked at the back of Rallo's head.

"Yes. That's what I heard. I swear it wasn't me."

"And you knew about this all along? So that's how you show me your loyalty?"

"Ish, I didn't get a chance to tell you because I had to go down south to see my grandmother. I swear, I was gonna drop a dime to you as soon as I touched down."

Ishmael, unimpressed, looked at one of his men and lifted his shirt, exposing the butt of the Glock that was shoved down the front of his jeans. His worker then removed his own hammer and stood behind Rallo.

"A'ight, Rallo, you done good, man. Real good," he said, walking back in front of Rallo. "I'm gonna let you go, but remember this, I don't like frontin'-ass niggas on my team." Ishmael was calm.

"I know, man. Thanks, Ish man. I swear you won't have no problems out of me. I'm gonna be the most productive worker you got on your team." Rallo breathed a sigh of relief.

"A'ight, cool," Ishmael said.

His worker was screwing the silencer on the gun as Ishmael and Derrick began to walk out of the room.

"Untie him and clean him up when you're finished," Ishmael said, not looking back as they exited the room.

"Thanks, Ish," Rallo yelled after him.

Before Ishmael and Derrick reached the front door, they heard the muffled shots echo.

Derrick and Ishmael had been cruising the streets checking on his blocks for about two hours.

"Ishmael, take me by Bev's crib. My sister needs a new refrigerator."

"A'ight. I was planning on getting up with Bev sooner or later anyway. I wanted to see if she knew anything about where we could catch up with the twins."

Derrick nodded and threw his toothpick out of the window and produced a fresh one from the top pocket of his shirt.

Ishmael watched him.

"Damn, man. What you got stock in them shits or something? You fuck around and get ptomaine poison," he said, laughing.

"Nigga, the way yo' ass be sucking on violet candy, I know you got a mouthful of rotten teeth by now," Derrick retorted.

"Naw, man, all thirty-two of my teeth are straight."

"Well then don't worry about what I'm doing, nigga. You the one walking around here smelling like a florist," Derrick cracked.

Ishmael smiled. He had been addicted to the violet candy for years. He'd planned to stop eating them because the candy did mess up the taste of food.

As the men rode in silence, Derrick began to notice Ishmael's unusual behavior.

"What's up, Ish?"

"I'm good."

"Come on and come wit' it," Derrick insisted.

Ishmael concentrated on his driving, not saying a word.

"You ain't gonna spit it? Keep it to yourself then. Keep it all bottled up and shit," Derrick said sarcastically as he looked out the window, twirling his toothpick.

"It's Zo," Ishmael blurted out.

"What about her?"

"I'm tired of her shit."

"Oh, you think?" Derrick responded nonchalantly.

"Save that shit, Rik. I'm just saying...I don't know, man."

"I know. I told you about her ass before. She ain't for you, Ish."

"Yeah, yeah, I heard all that shit before. But she the only down bitch I know," Ishmael stated.

"Down bitch? Ish, you talking out the side of your neck."

"I'm gonna give her one more chance to fuck up, and she's ghost." He tried to convince Derrick.

Derrick chuckled under his breath. "One more chance, huh?" he stated barely above a whisper.

"I'm for real this time, Rik."

"Oh, a'ight," Derrick said, still unimpressed.

Ishmael ignored him and continued driving in silence, his mind racing. He had so much tension building inside his body. Zola was becoming a pain in the ass. There was also the pressure from Leroy and the fact that he got robbed twice last month. *This shit has got to stop,* he thought.

In the game if a nigga in leadership position were caught slipping, he would be considered soft. If it was ever detected that his bitch had him wide open, then it showed a sign of weakness, leaving it open season for all the haters who laid in the cut waiting for him to fuck up.

Although Derrick was his boy, he couldn't trust anyone. Ishmael had seen it all his life. Partners in crime, do-or-die type niggaz on the come-up and when they did reach the top, greed would eventually take over, and before you knew it, there was a war among friends who at one time swore they would be doggs for life. That's just how it worked: business was business. Money, street credibility, and respect, without all three you ain't shit in the game.

Even though he discussed some things with Derrick, he had to make sure that Derrick didn't know how everything was affecting him because eventually, one day his right-hand man would be the one to fuck him.

They continued to drive in silence while Ishmael was in deep thought.

"Yo, Ish, you can have any bitch on the planet, and you pick ha gold-digging, sack-chasing ass," Derrick said, interrupting his thoughts.

"Naw, Rik, I don't trust none of these bitches. Shit, Zola is about the best one out here."

"Yeah, a'ight, nigga," Derrick stated, unconvinced.

"For real, man. There ain't no loyal bitches out there. They all want this paper I got."

They arrived on Eighteenth Avenue and pulled up in front of Beverly's house. She was sitting in her usual spot on the porch. Next to her sat her bottle of happiness. This time, unlike any other, she wasn't alone.

CHAPTER 10

LOVE AT FIRST SIGHT

The two women sat on the porch in the summer's night air. It wasn't so bad, Desiree thought. There were a lot of people out, but like Beverly said, they were on the corner and not in front of where she lived.

There were children running up and down the middle of the street playing while the older boys played football.

The women talked and talked, enjoying the cool breeze that came by once in a while. The mosquitoes were out something fierce. Beverly sent her son to the store to purchase some incense in order to fight off the hungry insects.

Night was starting to fall, and the streetlights that weren't busted out came on. Desiree lit up a Newport and bobbed her head to the music that was blaring from a boom box that sat on the curb.

A burgundy Lincoln Navigator pulled to the curb in front of the house where the women sat.

"Well I'll be damned, if it ain't Ish and Rik," Beverly stated.

"Who?" Desiree inquired.

"Rik and Ish. You remember them, right? They big time, Rae-Rae. You use to cop from they crew."

The two men exited the vehicle and made their way toward the porch.

"What do I owe this pleasure, gentlemen?" Beverly asked, exposing her rotting teeth.

"What up, Bev?" Ishmael asked.

Derrick just nodded. Ishmael saw someone he knew down the street. He turned on his heels and headed toward the corner.

Desiree watched him walk away. She was intrigued by his physique. She thought he was quite handsome and felt somewhat attracted to him. She shook the thought off as her true love, Bilal, jumped into her mind. She remembered she'd vowed to never love another. She would remain celibate until she died. She felt he was always in her heart and was watching over her.

"Yo, Bev, let me holla at you for a minute," Derrick commanded.

Beverly stepped down off the porch to talk to Derrick. The two walked over to the truck for their conversation. Desiree felt out of place. Now that she knew those were the dealers she use to purchase her drugs from, she suddenly felt that familiar funny feeling in her stomach.

Ishmael finally returned from the corner and approached Beverly and Derrick as they talked. He looked up onto the porch and caught Desiree's eye. She lowered her head, not wanting him to catch her staring at him.

Ishmael took that as his cue to approach the porch. "What's up, lady?"

"Hey," she said, not looking into his eyes.

"I never saw you around here before."

"I'm not from around here. I just got into town, and I'm staying with Bev for a little while."

Ishmael eased his way up onto the porch and sat next to her. Her heart began to beat faster, causing her to light up another cigarette.

"You shouldn't be smoking. It's bad for you," he said, looking at her, trying to make eye contact. "Yo, Rik, ask Bev about the twins Ron and Don," he shouted.

Derrick nodded and kept talking to Beverly. Ishmael returned his attention to Desiree.

Once he got a better look at her, he thought she was gorgeous. Her eyes were off the hook. She looked familiar to him, but he couldn't remember where he had seen her. It was those eyes that had him thinking he'd seen her before.

"What's your name?" he asked.

"Desiree."

"I like that," he crooned. "My name is Ishmael."

"Nice to meet you," she said, still trying to avoid eye contact.

"How long are you going to be staying here?"

"Not long, I hope."

"You hope? What do you mean?"

"Well, I'm going to school, and once I get a good job, I'll be getting my own place," she said, finally looking into his eyes.

"Oh, that's what's up. I like a woman who wants to further her education. I feel you," he said, putting on the charm.

"Let's ride, Ish," Derrick said.

"A'ight." He waved. "So do you got a man?"

"Yes, I have a man," she stated proudly.

"Well, what kind of a man is he if you're staying with Bev? If you was my lady, you would have your own shit," he said, standing.

"Well you're not my man," Desiree said with a little attitude.

"I'm just saying. Where he at?"

"He's around," she said, not wanting to tell her personal business to a stranger.

"You have a good night lady," he said, descending the steps.

His whole persona was becoming overwhelming. She felt hot flashes. His smile was worth a million dollars.

Beverly sat back down in her spot on the stoop, and both women watched the two men as they drove off.

"Hey, ho, I seen you and Ish up here kickin' it." Beverly looked at her with a smirk.

"No, sweetheart, don't get it twisted. We were just talking. Ain't nothing jumping off this way." Desiree stared at her.

"Why not?"

"Because I have a man."

"Who, Bunchy?"

"Yeah Bunchy." Desiree rolled her eyes.

"Please. Rae-Rae, Bunchy is dead. Are you going crazy?" Beverly said a little too loud for Desiree.

She began to look around to see if anyone had heard Beverly's statement.

"So much for all your sympathy," Desiree shouted, offended.

"I'm sorry, Rae-Rae, but listen to yourself. Bunchy is gone on home now, and you can't stop living because of it. If he were alive, I'm sure he would tell you to go on with your life. He was just that type of a man."

"I can't do it, Bev. I never had any closure with him. I feel like he's still very much alive and watching my every move to see my loyalty."

Beverly looked at her with unsure eyes.

"Rae-Rae, what the hell are you saying? Ain't no coming home for Bunchy, girl..." Beverly cut her sentence short after realizing that Desiree was straight tripping.

"Listen, Bev," Desiree said, interrupting her friend's thoughts. "I know it sounds crazy, but you don't understand...hell, I don't even understand. It's...it's just a feeling that I have. I feel like I would be cheating on him. You know what I'm saying?"

"Rae-Rae, you can sit here and dry up if you want. Bunchy ain't never coming home. You're gonna waste your life. Shit, by the time you realize what's going on, you gon' be old as dust and all dried up and shit."

Desiree sat heavy in thought. Although she wasn't elated by the way Beverly dissed Bilal, she believed Beverly was just drunk and couldn't comprehend.

While in prison, she had promised Bilal she would hold him down, even though he told her in many of his letters to move on with her life. She just couldn't do it. Bilal had taught her so much, and she wanted to be his ride-or-die chick. But she often wondered how far did a woman go when doing the bid with her man. Even if the man was dead.

"I'm saying, Rae-Rae, alright I feel you. I know you love him and want to be there for him, but he's gone. Keep him near and dear in your heart, but at least move on with your life. You're a beautiful woman, and you can just about do anything you want. Why waste it grieving over a man who's been dead for more than two years?"

Beverly finished off her bottle, tapping the bottom as if more would magically appear.

Desiree watched her do this. She often wondered how Beverly could drink so much. She couldn't imagine her feeling any different after drinking. Beverly seemed to be drunk all the time, even when she wasn't drinking.

"But to be straight with you," she blurted out loudly, scaring Desiree, "I would be doing me if I were you." Beverly tossed the bottle into the bushes. "And if a fine mafucka like Ish was pushing up on me? She-it, I would be on his ass like white on rice."

"Bev, he's a baller, and like I told you before, I need to stay away from that shit."

"Damn, Rae-Rae. You ain't gotta get high to be with him. That mafucka is laced. Do you here what I'm saying to you? That mafucka right there is your ticket outta the ghetto."

"No, Bev, I'm gonna go to school and get my own ticket out."

"Yeah, alright, be stupid if you want to," she said, taking one of Desiree's cigarettes without asking.

Beverly continued to try and reason with Desiree, but it was of no use. Desiree had her mind made up. She was going to stick to the script.

Desiree laid in her bed thinking about the knowledge that Bilal held. He was smarter than the average man. Bilal was so intelligent that people would come up to their apartment to get high and listen to his philosophy. The young boys from the corners would come up to their apartment to bag up or just plain take a break just to listen to Bilal's wisdom.

CHAPTER 11

WISDOM

One night one of the local runners name Luke came up to the apartment. Desiree sat on the living room floor, scraping residue from the pipe, and Bilal sat rocking back and forth on the sofa. He was sick and needed a fix bad. They had no money and no means of a hustle to cop. Bilal wasn't a thief, and he refused to allow Desiree to sell her body for it like the other drug-abused women did. As he sat on the sofa feeling like he wanted to vomit and shit at the same time, there was a knock at the door. His body ached so badly he could barely walk over to it. Finally reaching the door, he opened it and let the young boy in. He shivered and held his stomach, hoping the boy was there to do business and pass off a little something to him.

"Wisdom, what's good?" the boy shouted as he walked into the apartment, calling Bilal by the name some of the boys had given him.

"What's up?" Bilal asked.

"I need to bag up some product. Is it a'ight?"

"Yeah sure, come on in. You got something for me, right? You know there's a fee to use my place," Bilal stated, trying to keep himself from regurgitating in front of the boy.

"Fo' sure, Wisdom. You know I got you."

Bilal and Desiree charged anyone who came into their apartment no matter what they came to do in order to support their habits. They only received a small amount of money and food stamps each month from welfare for Bilal who was on permanent disability from the state.

He received the benefits because one day while picking up trash from the streets another employer who was driving the street sweeper drove over his foot, breaking several bones and dislocating his ankle, which caused him to walk with a permanent limp. He sued the city and received a large settlement. He was placed on permanent disability and had not worked since.

Luke handed Bilal two tiny baggies that contained the heroin. Bilal's hand shook as he took it from the boy.

"Luke, you can't do no better than this, man? I'm on E, and this ain't gonna do nothing but take the edge off a little. Shit, I'm gonna need at least three to get me off E," Bilal said.

Two bags was not enough to curb the sickness, let alone get Bilal of E.

Luke looked at him, and he could see the sickness in Bilal's face. He reached in his pocket and passed him two more bags.

Bilal rushed over to the kitchen table and sat down, preparing to sniff the off-white substance. At that point Desiree knew that Bilal needed dope more then she needed another hit, so she didn't say anything. Bilal snorted the first bag. Ten minutes later, he was feeling the effect of the dope. He could feel the pain subsiding in his legs.

"You know, youngun, I remember the time when dope was good. Yeah, those were the good old days."

Luke looked up at him. "I wouldn't know about that, man."

"There was a time when all you had to do was hit a half bag and that shit would have you in a gangsta lean that no pimp could acquire. Niggaz would be leaned so far into their nod that they could suck their own dick if they wanted to," Bilal drawled.

"Yo, Wisdom, why you snort this shit? Most people that cop from me shoot it up."

"I'm scared of needles. I could never see myself sticking a needle in my arm," Bilal said as he snorted the second bag.

"So have somebody else do it."

"Shit, that's worst than me doing it to myself. No, youngun, I *ain't wit' that."*

"I heard you get a better high when you shoot it."

"It's the same high, kid."

The young boy continued to bag his product while Bilal polished off the third bag. Bilal talked and talked for ten minutes, then he went silent, and his head nodded forward in slow motion.

Luke watched Bilal nod. He looked at the cigarette that Bilal held between his fingers, which had burned down to the filter

"Did you know, youngun?" Bilal stated, wiping spit from his mouth and putting out the cigarette on the floor. "Did you know that the government got a plan for us?"

"Oh yeah? What kind of plan?"

"They got a plan to get rid of all us poor niggaz," Bilal schooled.

"How you figure, Wisdom?"

"The way I see it, they let so much of this shit come into our country. Oh sure, they show you on the TV how they busted a couple of ships bringing the shit over every now and then, but that's just for show. The government is getting a cut off all that shit."

"Get the fuck outta here with that shit, man. How you figure they getting a cut?"

"See you young knuckleheads don't know shit, but I'm about to school you."

"Knock yourself out, Wisdom. School me."

Bilal went into another nod, and Luke kept working, waiting for him to come out of it.

"See, they working with them fuckers over in the other countries who actually produce this shit. They pay them mafuckas to make this shit. How you think them po' asses in other countries can afford to have labs and shit to produce this shit? Huh?"

"I don't know, Wisdom," Luke said, never looking at him.

"The government, nigga. That's how." Bilal scratched his chin then his neck, all in slow motion with his mouth shaped like an up-side-down frown.

"Yeah, they get a cut off that shit. They bring that shit over here and sell to the top suppliers for a good price. Then the suppliers sell it to their suppliers and then it keeps trickling on down to you mafuckas. And the government gets a cut off everybody. They making a killing in profits," Bilal announced.

Luke chuckled. "Where you get all this shit from, man?"

"It's a known fact, kid, a known fact."

"A'ight, Wisdom, I'm out. I'll catch up with you later." Luke stood. He grabbed up his product and shoved it in his pocket. Bilal shook his hand and went into another nod. Luke walked out of the apartment.

CHAPTER 12

DIE TRY N

THREE WEEKS LATER

"Tell the truth. You was up in that joint spankin' off, right?" Damon asked.

"Hell no, nigga," Niles protested.

"Yo, what y'all niggaz talking about?" Ishmael asked as he and Derrick approached a few of his runners. "Oh, what up, Niles? When you get home?" Ishmael asked, noticing he was standing there.

Niles used to be one of his most faithful employees—until he got busted. He took a charge for aggravated assault and drug distribution and had been released early from a five-year sentence.

"I got back last night. What up, Ish?" He extended his hand for a shake.

"Word? What, you got out on good behavior or some shit?" Ishmael asked.

"No. That nigga got out early for taking back shots from the Cos," Damon exclaimed.

Everyone burst into laughter. Some of the boys were jumping up and down and running in circles.

"Yo, fuck you, man," Niles shouted.

"Yo, y'all leave my man alone. So since you're back, you need some work?" Ishmael inquired.

"Hell yeah. I'm ready, man."

"Look at you. You always been my nigga." Ishmael smiled a proud grin. Damon looked on with suspicious eyes.

"Let me talk to you for a minute," Ishmael stated, draping his arm around Niles' shoulder and leading him off to the side.

"What that be about?" Damon inquired to Derrick.

"Yo, stay in your place," Derrick stated as he walked off behind Niles and Ishmael.

Damon looked after Derrick with piercing eyes. Damon had been down with Ishmael since the beginning, hoping to finally one day get promoted to a top position. He walked off, heading for the store, when Ishmael called him.

"Yo, D, where you headed?"

"To the store. I'll be back," he shouted.

Ishmael, Niles, and Derrick kicked it for a few minutes until Damon returned. Ishmael told Niles he would send something his way in a few hours and that he would talk to him later. Damon walked off with the two men, and they got into Derrick's GMC Yukon Denali. Once inside the truck Ishmael began to speak to Damon.

"Yo, D, now that Niles is back on the block, I need you to get him back on his feet. Make that run to the spot and pick him up a little something. I want you to start him off small and watch him," Ishmael stated, popping a piece of violet candy in his mouth.

"Watch him for what? You said that nigga was yo' boy and shit. What, you don't trust him?" Damon inquired with jealousy.

Ishmael looked over at Derrick, and they both snickered.

"Damn, man," Ishmael stated, disappointed.

"I'm saying… What's up, Ish?"

"Listen, man, that nigga just came home from the joint. He only did two of his mandatory five. For the charge he caught, something don't smell right. I'll give any nigga half a chance to fuck himself. I need you to keep an eye on that mafucka until I can peep his game. A'ight?"

"Yeah, a'ight, Ish. I feel you."

"That mafucka got to earn his spot back," Derrick said.

Later that night, Ishmael and Derrick swung by Beverly's house to pay her for the refrigerator she had gotten for Derrick's sister. She hadn't found anything out about Ron and Don, the dudes who Rallo snitched on, so Ishmael asked her about Desiree. Beverly told him that she had gotten a job at the IHOP in Elizabeth and was working at night.

"Oh word? She work at the IHOP, huh?"

"Yeah. She couldn't take it sitting around here at night. She said she was bored outta her mind," Beverly stated.

"So, Bev, what's up with your girl?"

"Who, Rae-Rae? She a'ight, Ish. Why, you wanna push up?"

"I'm just tryna peep her game," he said modestly.

"You better chill. If you start fucking around with Rae-Rae and that African bitch of yours find out, she gonna put some roots on yo' ass." Beverly laughed.

"You trippin', Bev. Don't no bitch run me. But I'm saying what up with yo' girl? She told me she had a man."

Beverly laughed. "If you want to call that a man. Please, that motherfucker died over two years ago."

"Oh word? Wait a minute, so why she fronting?"

"Um...she kinda still in mourning," she said.

"Mourning?"

"Yeah. Her long-time boyfriend died in prison."

"Oh, ha man was in prison? For what?" Ishmael inquired.

"His ass was doing life."

"Dayum," Ishmael and Derrick shouted at the same time.

"Hell yeah. Don't y'all remember that big-ass robbery about five years ago?"

"What robbery?" Derrick asked.

"Come on. Y'all mafuckas don't remember the couple who ran up in Groovers and tried to take Harry's fat ass out?" She looked at them sideways.

"Oh yeah! Yeah," Ishmael expressed.

"Well that was Rae-Rae and Bunchy who did that shit," she said as she hocked spit to the ground.

"Damn, Bev, you nasty," Ishmael stated in disgust.

"Who the fuck is Bunchy?" Derrick interjected.

"You know Bilal...Bunchy? Some called him Wisdom?" Beverly said.

Both men sat in thought, trying to place the names and a face.

"Where he rested at?" Derrick asked.

"Over there on Fifteenth Avenue," she responded. "He hung out with that nigga Roc who got smoked years back."

Ishmael and Derrick looked at each other.

"I knew that nigga Roc, but I didn't know Bilal. So she was the broad that was caught up in that robbery shit, huh?" Ishmael inquired.

"Yep, that would be Rae-Rae," Beverly said proudly.

"She was frontin' like she all prissy and shit," Ishmael said.

He sat and thought about the conversation he and Desiree had just the month before. He still couldn't place where he'd seen her before. Her eyes were driving him crazy. He remembered hearing about the robbery, but he didn't know who did it. He thought about how she would be a real ride-or-die bitch. She did time and had the balls to try and rip off Harry, of all people. As much muscle as Harry had, nobody in their right mind would fuck with him.

The more he thought about it, the more he was turned on. He had to get with Desiree—or he was going to die trying. Something about her turned him on.

Derrick got a call on his cell phone as they pulled away from the curb. It was Little Cash letting him know they knew where the twins were. Ishmael told Little Cash to get on the horn and call the crew to meet them at the spot for a meeting.

"I can't put my finger on it, but I seen shorty somewhere before," Ishmael stated out of nowhere.

"If she's hanging with Bev, then she ain't nothing but a chicken head," Derrick said, unimpressed.

Changing the subject, Ishmael said, "I been thinking about promoting D. What you think?" He really wasn't up for Derrick's arrogant remarks.

"That would be a a'ight move. That's one little nigga that be on the grind. Word, that's a good look," Derrick agreed.

They pulled up in front of the old tattered house and entered. All were already present, sitting around smoking Purple Haze. The men were laughing and joking.

"Yo, that bitch was serving me up something lovely. Shit, that bitch had my dick *and* nuts in her mouth. All that shit, yo," one male shouted.

"Get the fuck outta here," a couple of the guys yelled.

"Who he talking about?" Ishmael inquired.

"He talking about Funky Felicia."

Funky Felicia was a local girl who would let anybody hit it for money.

Rumor had it that her body odor was foul.

"*Ill*, that shit is nasty. You let that dirty bitch put ha mouth on your shit?" Ishmael asked, frowning.

"Hell yeah, he did. That bitch twat stink so bad, she could clear out a baseball stadium full people," another male joked.

The room erupted with laughter.

"Man, stop playing. She don't smell that bad," the boy defended.

"Dude, that bitch pussy stink, man." Derrick interjected.

"A'ight. A'ight," Ishmael announced. "The Haze got y'all niggaz in here trippin'."

Ishmael got the rest of the information from Little Cash, and they got down to business. They were going to move in on the twins' the next night and all meet up at the garage when they had them caught. The men sat around for another hour smoking and cracking jokes on one another while Ishmael sat back and thought about Desiree.

CHAPTER 13

LOST

Desiree dragged herself into the apartment. She was so tired and her feet hurt. She went straight to her bedroom. She didn't want anything to eat nor did she have the energy to take a shower.

She fell face first onto her bed and closed her eyes.

"You ain't even gonna wash your ass?" Beverly asked, standing in the doorway.

Desiree sat up in the bed, rubbing her eyes.

"I wasn't, but since you put it that way, I guess I need to."

"Yes you do, but not before I tell you the low down." Beverly hopped on the bed with her.

Desiree smiled at Beverly. There was never a dull moment with her. She always had gossip to tell, and there was never a time when she didn't have anything to say.

"Girl," she drawled, "Ish and Rik came by here last night, and guess what?"

"What, Bev?" Desiree asked, not really wanting to know.

Since she'd seen Ishmael, she couldn't shake him from her thoughts. Before she started working, she and Beverly would sit on the porch every night taking in the scenery. Every time a burgundy truck would drive down the street, her heart would flutter like a schoolgirl in love. It was getting to the point she was silently wishing he would come back around.

Eventually she decided to get a job. She really needed the money, but most of all, she needed to get him off her mind.

"Ish asked about you."

Beverly sat back and waited for Desiree to respond, but she didn't. "Did you hear what I said, Rae-Rae?"

"Uh, yeah."

"So do you want to know what he said?"

"Not really, but I know you're going to tell me anyway."

"Girl, he want to push up."

"He's not my type, Bev."

"Your type? Shit, a paid nigga like that is any bitch's type. You trippin', Rae-Rae."

"Bev, I don't want to talk about this right now. I'm tired. I'll talk to you later about it."

Beverly shook her head in disappointment. "You better let go of Bunchy, Rae-Rae. You need to move on with your life, and if a paid nigga like Ish wants to get down, then you need to get with him," she stated, leaving the room and closing the door behind her.

Desiree took her shower and went to bed. She lay in her bed, not able to fall asleep. She thought about Ishmael. Should she go on with her life? She felt the need to be loyal to Bilal, no matter what. Since she started working at IHOP, she had begun to save her money. Beverly was nice enough not to charge her rent, but Desiree still gave her something every week she got paid. The rest she put away. She was saving to get her own apartment. She would be starting school in the fall, and she needed to move into her own place.

Just the other day when she was coming up the stairs to the apartment, she smelled the familiar scent of burning cocaine. Her stomach began to bubble, and the anticipation of getting high ran all through her body. She could almost taste it, but she pushed forward and went into the apartment.

As she lay on the bed, she reminisced about when she first met Bilal as she slowly drifted off to sleep.

Desiree met Bilal at Don Pepe, a Portuguese restaurant downtown. At the time, she was an outside sales representative for a international computer software company. The software business was booming, and Desiree raked in more than seven grand a month in sales alone, not including her sixty-thousand-dollar-a-year salary. She created her own hours and drove a company car. The company also supplied her with a cell phone, credit card and an expense account. She traveled back and forth from California to Florida. She enjoyed her career and had the ambition to become a partner in the business. At the age of twenty-four, she had it going on.

Desiree and two of her coworkers pulled up into the restaurant parking lot. The valet opened her door, and she stepped out. Her lean legs were exposed by the split that ran up the front of her skirt. The young attendant eyed her smooth legs with hunger. He placed a ticket into her hands and looked away shyly as she locked eyes with him for gawking at her legs. The women strutted toward the restaurant. After being seated, they all ordered their drinks and began to discuss the latest gossip.

After lunch Desiree signed the receipt for the bill, charging their lunch to her expense account. She leaned back in her chair and smoked her cigarette. The women continued to talk and giggle freely. They each were a little tipsy from the two pitchers of sangria they had consumed. Desiree excused herself to go to the ladies' room.

Once leaving the ladies' room, she stepped out of the door and ran smack into a tall gentleman. He grabbed her to keep her from falling, apologized to her, and asked if she was okay. At first she was angry because she was almost tossed to the floor from the collision—until she looked up into his handsome face. She blushed and excused herself, walking briskly back to her table.

Bilal went back to the bar where he sat with friends. He watched her the whole time she remained there. They made eye contact, and he smiled at her, but she wouldn't hold his eyes for long before turning away.

Desiree and her coworkers made their way into the parking lot to retrieve their cars. Desiree walked over to hers and got in. She put the key into the ignition, and someone tapped on her window, causing her to scream. She looked up, and it was Bilal.

"Are you crazy?" she yelled.

"No. I didn't mean to scare you. I'm sorry. I didn't want you to leave with the possibility of me never seeing you again."

She stared into his almond-colored eyes and melted.

From that moment on, they were inseparable. Desiree loved everything about him. She believed he was her soul mate. He was ten years her senior, and his experience turned her on. The knowledge Bilal held was unbelievable. Desiree couldn't understand why he wasn't some type of professional businessman. He was a city trash worker. He made pretty good money, but Desiree felt he had much more intelligence than to settle for a city job.

They dated a few months, and Bilal moved into her quaint two-bedroom townhouse.

One day she came home from work and Bilal was sitting on the sofa with the remote in his hands. He appeared to be falling asleep. His head fell forward in slow motion. The remote was hanging on the edge of his fingertips, and a cigarette clung to the corner of his mouth. The ash that protruded from the end of the cigarette had reached the length of the cigarette itself. It had not been plucked since its lighting.

Desiree stood in front of Bilal, watching him. He never sensed her presence. She called out to him, and he jerked his head and the ash fell from the cigarette. The excuse he gave her was that he was really tired and had a hard day at work. This incident and other signs were evidence of Bilal using heroin.

Eventually his addiction was exposed. Instead of her nipping the sticky situation in the bud, she accepted his crutch because the love she had for him wouldn't allow her to leave him.

She found herself being jealous of the relationship he had with heroin and wanted to be a part of it, thinking it would bring them even closer. However, Bilal knew how deadly the drug was. He knew that a dope addict's life was a living hell on earth, and he couldn't see his queen, the woman who accepted him out of love, ever experiencing the downfall that came with using.

But Desiree, being the stubborn, demanding woman she was, kept insisting. With the pressure on, he had no other choice, so he introduced her to cocaine. She snorted the substance until she no longer could acquire a proper high. That's when she graduated and joined the millions of others in the world of crack.

CHAPTER 14

DOUBLE TROUBLE

Most of the squad met at the garage at the same time. They were following out their plans as scheduled. Damon had called Ishmael twice the night before, stating he spotted one of the brothers, and he had a clear shot to take him out, but Ishmael had to let him know that he needed to be patient, and they were going to stick to the script.

The garage was an old mechanic shop that sat next to an empty lot. The owner of the shop was Derrick's uncle who used to fix cars. Now he was too old to fix himself a cup of tea.

Long ago he had let Derrick have the shop with hopes that he would carry on the long line of mechanics who were in the family. Derrick led his uncle to believe that's what he was doing. He did so by letting The Mob Squad come to the shop to work on their personal cars, but in reality it was their meeting place. They'd done everything including decapitating bodies, planning their strategies for upcoming jobs, screwing broads on the second floor in the garage's bedroom, and just lounging around.

All in attendance were wearing black gloves. They gathered around the two brothers who they had placed at the saw table, which was nailed to the floor. Each of the twins' legs were roped to the table's legs, and their bodies were tied to their chairs. Their hands were placed securely in the vice grips that sat in front of them. The vice grips were mounted to the table in front of them.

Their mouths were duct taped, and they were blindfolded. They were drenched in sweat, fearing the worst. They jerked their heads simultaneously in different directions detecting all in the room.

Ishmael removed the blindfold from Ronald first and instructed one of the men to remove the one from Donald's eyes. The look on both the men's faces were identical— horrified.

"What's up, fellas?" Ishmael stated, smiling down at both of them.

Ronald tried to speak first, but his words were muffled. Ishmael ripped the tape brutally from his mouth, causing the man to scream.

"Ish man, what's going on?"

"What's going on? What's going on is my money, nigga."

"What money, Ish?"

"Here we go with the same ole bullshit. Listen, I ain't even sweating the money no more. It's the G.P., nigga. I'm setting an example for mafuckas like you two. Don't fuck with Ishmael's shit," he stated in his usual calm demeanor.

Donald began making loud noises like he had something to say, so Ishmael ripped the tape from his mouth as well. Ronald and Donald both began to speak at the same time.

"Yo, shut the fuck up. You had your turn. I'm finished with you," Ishmael yelled at Ronald.

All who gathered in the garage were now alert, if they weren't before. Ishmael was not a yeller. He was not one to lose his patience easily, but when he did, watch yo' back.

Ishmael looked at Donald, giving him the opportunity to speak.

"Listen, Ish—" he said, taking a deep breath, "I know what you thinking, but listen, man, Rallo said we was gonna hit this small-time nigga. On everything that I love, we had no idea that it was yo' shit, man," he pleaded.

"Just like I thought, you ain't got shit to say either. Yo, check this out, Rallo's breathing dirt right now. There ain't no coming back for Rallo. So y'all can kill that shit. You feel me?" Ishmael growled at the two of them.

"Yo, Ish man. Listen, man," Donald yelled.

"We got the money. Just give us time to go get it," Ronald finished the sentence.

"Picture that shit. Silence them niggaz," Ishmael yelled as he walked away from the table.

Duct tape was reapplied to the men while Ishmael paced the garage floor for several minutes, trying to get his head together. He wanted to pull his burner out and pop both of them in the dome with one single bullet each, but that wouldn't be satisfying enough for him. They wouldn't suffer. No, he wanted them to suffer. He stared furiously at the two men.

The twins whimpered and cried, trying to break free. Damon began to have a little fun with the men by teasing them and punching them in the face.

Derrick pulled a box of two-inch thick-as-nails straight pins that he had taken from his sister's sewing kit from his pocket. He held up the box and shook it at Ishmael, getting his attention. It was as though Derrick had read Ishmael's mind. Ishmael smiled and took the box from his friend's hands.

"Blindfold them fuckas," Derrick instructed.

When the blindfolds were applied. Ishmael showed the men what he wanted done without opening his mouth and saying a word. He didn't want his victims to know what was about to happen to them. Damon jumped up in front of Ishmael with his hand held out, letting him know he wanted to put in work, so Ishmael gave him a handful of pins and the other half to Little Cash.

One by one the men jabbed the straight pins underneath the fingernails of the twins. One member held one chair while another held the other chair to keep it from rising off the floor.

The duct tape did nothing to muffle the sounds of shrills and screams that came from the men. Derrick turned on the garage's stereo system with surround-sound speakers to drown out the screams. Ishmael looked over at two of his crew members, Dice and Nate. They kept turning theirs heads as the pins where inserted into the twins fingers. Ishmael laughed to himself thinking how these two dudes would body a nigga in a New York minute but couldn't watch the scene.

As each pin was inserted, blood squirted everywhere. Ronald began to fart and defecate on himself, and each time he did this, Damon would ram another pin in him while he taunted him.

"You punk-ass mafucka, shitting on yourself. You ain't think about that shit when you was parlaying with Ish's money, did you? Huh? Mmm," he said after each pin he inserted.

Satisfaction was written all over Ishmael's face. Donald was in so much pain he passed out.

"Hold up. This mafucka passed out," Little Cash stated.

Click, another member of the crew, cracked Donald across the face with his gun, awakening him. Click acquired his name for being known to empty an automatic weapon and keeping his finger on the trigger well after the rounds where discarded, causing the clicking noise.

After being cold copped with the gun, Donald came to and began to scream as realization of the pain from the pins hit him again.

Ishmael instructed the two men to pull out the pins. From the way the twins screamed, you couldn't tell which was worst, putting the pins in or taking them out. Damon pulled out the pins in slow motion, enjoying the pain.

Ishmael noticed that Derrick was irritated with the whole scene. He knew torture was not Derrick's forte and that he only tolerated it to please him. With frustration settling in, Derrick pulled out his knife and stood behind Ronald. He grabbed Ronald's forehead, pulling it back, and slit his throat. Derrick held on to Ronald's head and allowed the blood to back up in his throat.

Ronald began to gurgle and choke on his own blood. After his body stopped twitching, Derrick let go of Ronald's head, and it fell forward with his chin resting on his chest.

Everyone looked on with amazement. Ishmael shrugged and walked over to a shocked Donald.

"Hey, Don," he shouted to get his attention. "See you in hell, baby."

Ishmael then turned to Nate and Dice. "Slump his ass." He instructed them to do what they do best.

"After you, man," Nate said, extending his hand.

"No, by all means, after you," Dice returned the courtesy.

The two men spoke like they were English chaps.

"Much oblige to you, my friend," Nate said and pumped Donald in the neck with a bullet.

Dice then completed the job by popping a bullet to Donald's eye. Damon was laughing hard. He thought they were the funniest thing since BET *Comic View*.

Ishmael and Derrick's work was done.

"Chop 'em up and dump 'em," Ishmael instructed as he and Derrick left the garage.

Ishmael was silent while Derrick drove. It was 4:30 A.M. They rode through the blocks checking with each team's captain before moving on to the next destination.

"So what's up? You calling it a night or what?" Derrick inquired.

"Yeah. Take me home, man."

After pulling up in front of Ishmael's one-family home, Ishmael gave Derrick dap and hopped out of the truck. He watched Derrick round the corner, then turned and walked up his driveway. He pressed the automatic garage opener button on his key-chain remote, and the door opened to reveal his Lincoln Navigator Unlimited, his BMW K1200GT motorcycle, and his silver CLK320 Mercedes Benz. He jumped in his truck and backed it out of the driveway. Tapping the button again to close the door, he headed for IHOP to get a quick bite to eat.

CHAPTER 15

FOOD FOR THOUGHT

Desiree was taking her break in the back room of the IHOP restaurant. She had been there for five hours, and she was beat. She still had a few hours to go before punch-out time. She didn't get much sleep because of all the noise that went on in the apartment. Beverly's kids ran in and out of the house, slamming the door constantly, and every time they slammed the door, Beverly would yell at them.

"What the fuck is wrong with y'all niggaz? Y'all know Rae-Rae in there tryna sleep."

As if it wasn't bad enough that they made noise, the neighbors were yelling in the hallways or outside in front of the house, so most of the time she only got a few hours of sleep.

She sat in the chair at the table with her head on her forearms. She had asked her coworker Darrell to wake her up at the end of her break.

Meantime, Ishmael pulled into the parking lot of the restaurant. He sat there for a few moments contemplating whether he should go in. He didn't know if Desiree was working or not. Finally deciding to take the chance, he got out of the vehicle.

Walking into the restaurant he headed to the front register.

"Welcome to IHOP. Table for one?" the woman asked.

Ishmael nodded, wondering why she would ask that question when he was the only one standing there. The waitress grabbed a menu and a place mat and asked him to follow her.

"Right this way, sir," she beckoned.

Ishmael followed the tiny woman through the restaurant to a rear corner booth that sat two people.

Ishmael sat down and looked out the window at his truck. He had a good clean view of his baby.

"What would you like to drink?" she asked.

"Um...I'll take a 7-Up," he stated while looking over the menu. "Um, excuse me, is Desiree working tonight?"

"Yeah, she here. She on break though," she said with a crooked smile.

"Well, I'll wait until she gets off break to order." He winked at her.

The waitress smiled. "Well in that case you need to sit over in her section." Ishmael moved over to the next row and continued to view the menu.

"Desiree, Desiree." Darrell shook her awake.

"Hmm."

"It's that time. You got three minutes left on your break," he stated.

"Okay," she said, rubbing her eyes. "Thanks."

She stood and took a deep stretch. Desiree went into the bathroom to rinse her mouth out and washed her face and hands. Exiting the bathroom, she swiped her employee card, punching in from break. As soon as she appeared at the station, the short waitress informed her that she had a customer.

Desiree rolled her eyes at the hostess. She knew she was on break, so why would she seat a customer at her section?

There were two other couples in the restaurant. It was slow for a Friday morning. Their busiest nights were from Thursday to Sunday, and of course on the holidays. But that night seemed eerie. It was like a ghost town in the place. Normally Desiree liked it when it was slow, but that evening she needed to keep busy in order to stay awake.

"How long has he been here?" she asked while peering down at the customer who had the menu covering his face.

"He just got here."

Desiree snatched a piece of peppermint candy that sat in a bowl at the register. She grabbed her pad and pen and headed for the customer to see if he was ready to order.

"How are you today, sir? I am your waitress and my name is..." Desiree stopped in mid-sentence when Ishmael lowered the menu.

He looked up into her green eyes and smiled.

"What are you doing here?" she whispered to him, looking around to see if anyone was watching.

"Ordering me something to eat. What are you doing here?" he asked as if he didn't know she worked there.

"You know why I'm here. I'm working. As if you didn't know." She rolled her eyes, placing her hand on her hip.

"You work here?"

She sucked her teeth at him. "You know I work here. Don't play yourself."

"What a coincidence." He continued to smile at her.

Ishmael looked her up and down, almost undressing her with his eyes. She had on a pair of black fitted stretch pants that hugged her curves, a white low-cut shirt that showed her cleavage, and an IHOP apron.

She began to feel uncomfortable, and she tugged at her clothing.

"Are you going to order something or not?" she asked with attitude.

"Easy, Rae. I haven't decided yet," he toyed with her.

"Well, I'll come back when you're ready." She walked away.

Once back at the station, the short hostess approached her.

"Mmm, I see somebody got an admirer," she said, smiling.

"I don't know what you're talking about."

"Hmm. The way that baller was checking for you, I know you know what I'm talking about. Besides, he asked for you personally."

Desiree sucked her teeth and went to stand out of Ishmael's view. *These people are so damn nosy,* she thought.

"Go take his order. You can't keep a customer waiting all night." The short hostess snickered.

"Who y'all talking about?" the manager named Hazel asked, walking up to them.

"About that fine mother father sitting in Desiree's section."

Hazel looked in the direction the short waitress was pointing. "Hot damn! I'd like to ride his pony. Umm, umm, umm!" Hazel said with a little too much enthusiasm for a woman in her early fifties.

"I told her to get with him. He is all that. Plus, he asked for her personally." The tiny woman elbowed Hazel.

"A request, huh? What be your problem, gurl? You better nab that tenderoni." Hazel continued to gawk.

"Hazel, you just a horny old woman," the short hostess said, laughing.

"Call me what you want, but if baby gurl over here don't get with that, then he'll be calling the Lord's name laid out on his back by the time I'm done with him." She snapped her fingers.

Ishmael watched the women in their huddle and knew they were talking about him. He watched Desiree's disgusted expression as she stalked toward him.

"What's wrong, ma?"

"Nothing. What do you want?" she said, irritated.

"Now is that the way to treat a customer?" He smiled.

"Listen, Ishmael, I'm at work, and I don't have time for games."

"A'ight, ma, I see you're not in a playing mood. I'll have the steak and eggs," he said, placing the menu down on the table.

"How do you want your steak?" She sounded rehearsed.

"Let's see—" he took a sip of his soda—"well done."

"How would you like your eggs?" She rolled her eyes at him.

"Rae, I'm not here to cause you any trouble. I just want to talk to you."

"How would you like your eggs?" Her attitude reappeared.

"I want eggs whites only, scrambled well."

"Egg whites are extra."

"Do it look like I'm beat for money?" He leaned back, staring at her blankly.

"I don't know what you're beat for," she said, snatching up the menu and storming off.

Hazel watched the interaction and decided to take it upon herself to approach Ishmael's table.

Desiree watched Hazel from a distance, at the way she giggled and performed like a high school kid. Hazel was overweight and ghetto fabulous. Her big belly jiggled every time she laughed as she playfully hit Ishmael.

Several minutes went by while Desiree gawked as the two conversed. Hazel waddled her wide hips, adding a little too much swing to them over to Desiree.

"Desiree, I just had a conversation with your customer. He is quite the gentleman. He's informed me that he's been tryna talk to you for several weeks now and you won't give him the time of day. What's the problem?"

This pissed Desiree off that Hazel had the nerve to get all up in her business.

"First of all, Hazel, I'm a grown woman. Secondly, I don't need you in my business." Desiree rolled her eyes. "Lester, is that food ready yet?"

"Coming up in a minute, Desiree," Lester the cook shouted.

"Listen, Desiree," Hazel said, pulling her over to the side, "why don't you at least see what he wants? He really sounded sincere to me, and I can tell a player when I see one. He don't strike me to be a man of games. I think it would be a good look for you, gurl. Give the man a chance. If you not feeling him, then drop his ass like a bad habit, but at least try," Hazel reasoned.

"Why are you doing this?" Desiree asked.

"Doing what?"

"Helping me—you know, being nice to me."

Hazel looked off into the distance before she spoke again.

"Because you remind me of my little sister. She was just like you. I wanted nothing but the best for her, but she died at the age of twenty-five. Her life was taken for no good reason. She worked hard and went to school to better her life, just like you. I miss her, and when you got hired here, I felt a certain closeness to you because of her."

Desiree was taken back. She didn't know how to quite decipher what Hazel had just said to her. She couldn't understand what Hazel's sister had to do with her when they barely had conversations with each other while they worked. But for whatever reason she was doing this, Desiree felt she was sincere and she wanted to give Ishmael a chance to see what he wanted. But he was a drug dealer, and she wasn't having that. Although in the back of her mind, she longed for him secretly, she would never outright admit it to anyone—especially Beverly.

CHAPTER 16

HAD ENOUGH

Ishmael was sitting on his bed counting his money. Something wasn't right. He knew he had a certain amount that he kept on the shelf behind the wall panel.

"Sixty...eighty...Two thousand five hundred and eighty?"

He sat back and looked at the grip he held in the palm of his hand. He knew he kept an even five G's on his shelf for easy access—his "play money" is what he called it. He would replace any play money that he took at the end of each week. Lately he had been coming up short on his count. But he would just chalk it up to the amount of haze with which he had been indulging himself lately.

He opened his safe and put in the grip from the block he collected. He removed the money he had in his pocket and replaced that shy of his play money. He then put everything back in its original place and closed the safe, replacing the wall panel. When he came out of the closet, Zola was standing in the room. Ishmael was startled and pulled out his gun, aiming it at her.

She threw up her hands. "Shit, Ishmael," she yelled.

"Why the hell you creeping round here for?" he asked, jamming his gun back in his waistband.

"I wasn't creeping. I walked into the bedroom."

Ishmael walked back over to the bed and sat down to remove

his Timberlands.

"Where you been, Ish?" Zola asked.

"What you mean where I been?" He frowned at her.

"I mean what I said. Where you been?" She stood there with her hands on her hips.

"I been working. Where the hell you think I been?"

"You ain't never stayed out the way you have been the past few weeks. I hardly see you anymore."

He didn't say a word. He continued to get undressed quietly.

"So you not going to say anything?"

"Go 'head, Zo. I'm not for this shit today. I wanna try and get a few hours of sleep."

"Oh, I see what's up. You sticking another bitch?" She laughed. "You think it's sweet like that. But trust she can have yo' ass 'cause yo' shit is straight garbage anyway."

Ishmael looked up at her with evil eyes. "Trust, if I was *fucking* some-body else, yo' ass would be history. Although that don't sound like a bad idea." He smiled back at her. "If my shit is garbage then bounce."

Zola rolled her eyes at him and stormed out of the room. He laughed to himself. It felt good to see her being on the receiving end for a change. Although he wasn't sleeping with Desiree, he still enjoyed seeing the jealousy seep through Zola's pores.

It was 10:00 A.M. when he finally laid back on the bed after getting undressed. He had dropped Desiree off at home earlier that morning. Since that day two weeks ago in the restaurant, they had become quite close. They did a lot of talking. Nothing intimate yet, but a lot of good conversations came out of the time they spent together. Desiree also made it real clear that she didn't like his occupation of choice.

He would pick her up from work at the end of her 7:00 A.M. shift, and they would drive to her house and sit out front talking sometimes for hours. He adored her more each time they were together. She had street smarts and intelligence. Desiree had asked him on several occasions if he would leave the game and get a real job. He told her he'd plan to, but if she became his lady he would drop it like a bad habit, but he didn't even believe what he told her.

On one occasion she had asked him about his acquired taste for violet candy. He told her that it kept his breath fresh. She asked him if he wouldn't mind stop eating the candy. It reminded her of a day she'd like to forget. She didn't go into detail about it, so he stopped eating the candy although he had a certain addiction to it.

His feelings for Zola were giving way to the newfound friend he acquired in Desiree. The more he thought about her, the less he thought about Zola. He had asked Desiree out on a date that evening since she didn't have to work. She'd accepted his offer. He thought about the night's plans and went over them in his head.

Zola stormed back into the room, interrupting his thoughts.

"Ishmael, I need some money," she demanded.

He didn't respond.

"Do you hear me talking to you?"

"Zola, what do you need the money for?" he asked with a blank expression.

"I just need some money. You gonna give it to me or not?"

"Not." He smiled at her.

He watched her she stomped off again like a child not getting her way.

CHAPTER 17

THROWING SHADE

Damon pulled up in front of Burger King. His passenger door opened, and Zola got into the car.

Damon had always been sweet on Zola, but Zola always had plans for the big fish in the pond, Ishmael, so she used Damon to get to Ishmael. Zola knew all about how Damon kicked dirt on Ishmael. Ishmael always thought Damon was loyal to him, but Zola knew different.

"What's up, Zoey?" He smiled.

"Hi Damon," Zola said in her sexiest voice.

He pulled into the oncoming traffic. They rode in silence for a few minutes. Damon took several peeps at Zola's legs while driving.

She wore a jean miniskirt that had risen up to her upper thigh when she sat down. Her legs were shining as if she applied mounds of baby oil to them, giving them a sheen. Her muscular thighs showed their form, bulging each time she moved. His imagination ran wild as he wondered if she was wearing any panties.

"So what you been up to?" Zola asked, breaking him out of his daydream.

"You know me, I been on the grind."

"Yeah, I hear you." She looked over at him. "How's Ishmael been treating you?" she asked, not wasting any time.

"Well, you know how that is. I eat though."

"No, for real, D. What's really good?"

Damon clenched his jaws, not sure of where the conversation was going. He had always been sweet on Zola, but she hurt his feeling when she got with Ishmael. He thought they were going to hook up. He felt betrayed although they were never official.

"Why? What's up, Zoey?"

"I'm just tryna make sure you straight. You know how mafuckas can get when they getting that paper. They start acting like they above and beyond a nigga when *you* had his back all these years," she said, scheming.

"True, true," he agreed.

"And the fucked-up thing is, he be front'n on you when it comes time to pass out the promotion papers, you know?" she continued to toy with him.

Damon continued to drive, staring straight ahead, not saying a word. Zola knew she was getting to him, so she continued to push the knife farther into his back.

"How long you been down with Ishmael?"

"Like fourteen fucking years. Since I was like nine."

"Wow, nine years old? What could you have possibly been doing with him at nine?"

"At that time I lived on the same block with Ish. Back then he was a runner, and I used to run errands for him. Like going to the corner store or some shit like that. Them niggaz use to let me hang around with them. I was they lookout and shit. When Ish got put on his own blocks, he hired me as one of his main runners."

"So you saying that you was down with him at the very beginning?"

"Yeah, something like that," he said, looking like he was remembering those times.

"That's fucked up, Damon," she said, shaking her head.

"What?"

"I mean you was down with Ishmael from day one and you still a runner."

"Naw, Zoey, I ain't no runner. I got my own blocks," he stated proudly.

"Please, D, you ain't nothing but a runner—Ishmael's flunky." She sucked her teeth and rolled her eyes.

Damon pulled over to the side of the road and faced her. "Yo, what's up, Zoey?" He frowned.

"What?" she asked as if she didn't know what was going on.

"Stop bullshitting. What are you tryna say?"

"Alright, D," she said, facing him. "I got eyes. I see what's going on. Ishmael is treating you like shit. You should be his right hand man, not Derrick. You feel me?"

Damon sat there mean mugging her for a few seconds, trying to peep her game.

"Zoey, listen, I got territory that I run. I'm the *man* on my blocks. I got runners. Niggaz jump when I say. Do you feel *me*?"

"Yeah, I feel you. But do you know who the connect is? Do you go to the baller's meetings. Are you involved in any of the decision making?" she fired away.

"No," he said, turning away from her. He gripped the steering wheel, looking straight ahead.

"But you was down with him, watching his back since day one? And peep this," she said, not waiting for him to respond to her question. "What about when Ishmael got popped? Didn't you step up and run shit for him until he got home?" She already knew the answer.

Damon didn't respond. He swallowed hard and narrowed his eyes.

"D," she said, touching him lightly on the thigh, "I know you was heated with me when I stepped to Ish and dissed you, but I couldn't tell you what I was doing. I was only getting next to him so that I could infiltrate."

Damon looked at her with unsure eyes. "What?" He frowned.

"Let me put you down," she said, placing her hair behind her ear. "You were my best friend, and I respected you…and I still do. We use to have long hours of great conversations on the phone. I miss that. But I was on a mission for you, yo."

Damon raised his eyebrows.

"Yeah you," she said, confirming his curiosity.

"How you figure?" he asked.

"You should be the top man. Technically once Ishmael got sent up the river, the next man in line was you. So you should be da man, not him. But you were loyal, and you gave him his rank back, *and* you kept shit poppin' while he was gone."

She continued to stare at him, making sure she had his undivided attention before continuing. "I went on a mission to peep his game, and once I did that, I was going to bring it back to you so that you can take back what belongs to you. And baby," she said, moving her hand higher up his leg, "it's time."

"Time for what?" he asked, opening his legs wider, anticipating where she was going with her hand.

"It's time to get your spot back." She kept inching upward.

"And you think you capable of helping me pull that off?"

"Don't sleep, D. The safe is in his closet. I don't know the combination, but I'm sure you can get it open," she said as she stopped moving her hand. "Once you make Ishmael disappear, you gonna hafta get with that Herman Monster–acting nigga, Rik."

"I'ma hafta body Rik first then I'ma step to Ish. But I want the loot first. So how you plan on keeping him out of the house until I get the safe open?" he asked, placing his hand on hers and guiding it upward again.

His dick began to rise.

"You ain't heard? I'm nice with mine. Let me handled that part," she bragged, reaching her final destination.

"Oh yeah?" he whispered, enjoying her rubbing his hard-on.

"Oh yeah."

Zola unzipped his jeans and reached inside, pulling out what she had been searching for. She leaned over and spit on it and put it into her mouth, causing him to shiver.

Damon looked at the surroundings outside. It was broad daylight, and they were pulled over on a busy street. Seeing that no one was walking by, he laid his head back and enjoyed the best head he had had in a long time.

CHAPTER 18

LOSING FEELINGS

Ishmael stepped out of the shower. He wiped the mirror clean of the steam with his towel then peered into the mirror, looking at himself. He patted his body dry and pulled the clippers from the bottom cabinet and began to trim his sideburns and beard, edging them up a bit. His braids were fresh and intact. He had stopped by the African braid shop the day before to get them done. The braids were so tight that you could see the raised skin about his forehead. He could have easily gotten Zola to do them, but that was not even an option considering how she'd been tripping lately.

He checked the time on his cell phone, which was on the sink. It was 7:00 P.M. He had one hour before he went to pick Desiree up for their first date.

After he finished grooming himself, he walked into his closet to select his wardrobe. He stood in the middle of the closet with his arms folded across his chest, studying the attire that hung loosely about the thick plastic hangers.

He was taking Desiree to an industry party in the city for a famous rapper Diggy Mar. Everybody who was anybody was scheduled to be there.

It had been a long time since Ishmael had attended an industry party in the city. They became predictable and repetitious, and he basically outgrew them. It would be the same faces and the same drama. All the women walked around half naked and desperate, trying to find the nigga with the most paper.

They all had the same come-on line and all wore the same type of weave. One minute they would be up in a nigga's face, and if they didn't get a drink out of him, they'd move on to the next sucker. Ishmael could see right through the sack-chasing groupies.

But this night was different. The top suppliers were going to be at this party. They were to meet for a brief meeting about some new product that was just discovered over in Cuba. The word out was that the heroin was so pure that it almost looked yellow, and it was putting niggaz on they asses over in Cuba. Ishmael's main hustle was heroin, but he dealt in cocaine as well. The team wanted in, and Ishmael was a part of that team. If they got their hands on the product, they would surely rise above all. So all and all, this wasn't only a date. It was business as well.

Ishmael figured that after the meeting he would take Desiree to the Copa for some old-fashioned dancing and dinner. He had a hidden desire for dancing the salsa.

Several years ago Ishmael was sprung on this chick named Sasha. She was Spanish. She loved to dance the salsa. At first Ishmael thought the dancing was gay until Sasha taught him in the privacy of her home. They danced the sensual dance so much that after each lesson he and Sasha would end up butt naked on the floor.

He didn't quite know if Desiree would like dancing the salsa, but he damn sure was going to give it a try.

No one knew about that side of Ishmael except his ex-girlfriend Sasha, and he had intended to keep it that way—until now. He felt a certain type of closeness with Desiree, and he felt he was ready to share some of his secrets with her. Although they had not reached that point, now was as good a time as any to open up to her. Desiree made it clear how she felt about the game and all that came with it, and he told her he intended to stop.

He didn't know why she felt the way she did about the game, and he never asked. He figured when she was ready, she would tell him.

"Speak," Derrick yelled into the ringing phone.

"What up?" Ishmael responded.

"What's good? Where you at?"

"I'm swinging by to scoop up Rae. Where you at?"

"I'm sittin' in this fuckin' long-ass line waiting to go through the tunnel," Derrick complained.

"Oh, a'ight, I'll get wit' you when I get there."

"A'ight, one." Derrick disconnected the call.

He was sitting in traffic waiting to enter the Holland tunnel with Dice, Nate, and Click. Behind him a few cars back was Damon, Little Cash, and Niles. They were all going to the party, which was a treat for most of them. Ishmael would bring them on occasion whenever he went over to the city for a night of fun and relaxation. Although this was a business affair in a sense, no one knew that but Derrick. The rest were out for the night to chase skirts.

Before pulling off the block, Derrick instructed the knuckleheads riding in the car with Damon to go easy on the weed and to remember they was rolling with Jersey plates. Everybody carried a hammer, and he didn't need them doing anything stupid to get them busted. Damon stayed a few cars behind Derrick for a reason. He wasn't feeling taking orders from Derrick. Besides, he and Zola had some shit in store for him anyway.

The Acura Legend Damon drove was so clouded from them blowing trees, it was a wonder Damon could see anything driving. The base boomed from the large-watt speakers he had installed in the rear of the car, drawing major attention to the vehicle.

Ishmael pulled up in front of Beverly's house and blew the horn.

"Nigga, you better get the fuck out that Benzo and come see me," Beverly yelled, sitting back in the cut on the dark porch.

Ishmael turned off the engine and got out of the car. He adjusted the belt holding up his Armani pants, which he straightened over his Armani shoes.

He glided toward the porch.

"Hot damn! I hear you, my brotha. That's what's up, nigga," Beverly yelled, obviously impressed with Ishmael's ensemble. "And you pulled out the big dog tonight." She looked over at the Benz.

He gave a sly grin, knowing that he was doing his damn thing. "What's up, Bev?"

"Apparently you, nigga." She looked him up and down.

"Why you hiding out on the porch? Somebody looking for that ass, huh?" Ishmael joked.

"Is you crazy? I don't scare, and I definitely don't run from nobody."

"Where my girl at?"

"She upstairs." She pointed. "Rae-Rae! Ish down here for you," she yelled ghetto fabulous. "Go tell Rae-Rae Ishmael down here for ha," she told one of the kids running around. "So where y'all going?"

"To the city. Why? You rollin'?" He smiled, already knowing the answer.

"You know I can't go to the city. I got kids." She rolled her eyes at him, realizing he was toying with her.

Desiree walked onto the porch, and Ishmael looked at her. Although it was dark, he could still see her figure. She headed down the steps and stopped in front of him. The streetlights bounced off her radiant skin. She was wearing a black Chanel dress that fell above her knees. Its soft material lay upon her petite but shapely frame. The v-neck dove down the front of the dress, leaving room for her exposed cleavage. The sleeves of the dress dangled loosely, hanging to her elbows. Her hair was pinned up in a princess bun with long pieces hanging down around its crown.

"Aw, watch out now," Beverly yelled.

Desiree turned to Beverly. "Bev, be quiet. You are so loud."

"You look good, girl. Y'all make a nice couple," she said as if she was a proud parent at her daughter's prom.

Ishmael was in shock. He couldn't take his eyes off Desiree. Her legs were as smooth as a baby's ass and they shimmered in the night-lights. He held his hand out to her. She placed her manicured hand into the palm of his and stepped off the last step.

"All right now. Y'all have a good time," Beverly called out after them.

Desiree waved to Beverly and stepped into the Benz while Ishmael held the door open for her. He slid behind the wheel and started the engine. The aroma of Happy by Clinique filled the inside of the car. He took a whiff before pulling off.

Back at the club the crew pulled up to the valet. Everyone hopped out of the two vehicles. Damon practically fell out of the truck. Derrick stared at him and shook his head. He could see what was left of the smoke escaping out of all the open doors.

They all trailed behind him as he approached the front door. There were people standing in a line that wrapped around the building, seeming to never end. The chances of getting in were slim, but everybody wanted to get in to party with the stars and the ballers.

Derrick walked right up to the three bouncers who stood in front of the huge oak double doors. The combination of their muscles and them standing side by side exceeded the width of the doors. A short Italian man holding a clipboard stood looking like a dwarf in front of the men.

"Are you...on the list?" he asked, sounding nasally.

"Yeah," Derrick responded, detecting the cause of the little man's runny nose.

"Oh yeah?" He rubbed his red nose and sucked up mucus again. "What's the name?"

"Ishmael," Derrick advised him, looking over the top of the clipboard at the names on the list.

The man ran his finger down the list then he flipped to the second page and found the name he was looking for.

"Here it is. That's a party of nine." He rubbed his tearing eyes. "How many you got with you?" He looked around Derrick to see how many were in attendance.

"Seven," Derrick answered.

"Let them in," the man instructed the burly men standing behind him as he fidgeted with his collar.

They all walked in one by one. Damon was the last to go in.

"Just say no to drugs, man, damn," Damon exclaimed, walking past the little man. The rest fell out laughing and clowning the man.

Once inside the foyer of the club, each man was searched. No one brought their guns inside the club knowing there would be a search. They were allowed to keep their drugs but no weapons were allowed.

After being searched, they walked to the right at the end of the hall and got on a gated elevator. The music was loud but muffled. Once they reached the next level, the gate open. The music hit them in the face like the winds of a tornado. It was like stepping into an odyssey. They were souped, acting like kids in a toy store with a free shopping spree card. They disbursed and went their separate ways, chasing titties and asses that floated by them.

Derrick's demeanor never changed. He maintained the same gentle-giant appearance, focusing and surveying the room. Dice and Nate were right on his tail trailing him. They, too, maintained the stone faces with which they'd become quite comfortable. Although theirs eyes roamed the exposed flesh in which they came in contact, they kept their cool.

CHAPTER 19

GIFTED

As Ishmael drove, Desiree looked out the window. They both were silent, probably basking in their own thoughts. The radio was blazing WBLS FM's slow jams.

"You put it on tonight," he said, looking over at her.

She turned and looked at him with a smile. "You don't look so bad yourself." She winked at him.

Ishmael gave a bright smile. The Brothers Johnson's "Strawberry Letter 23" came out of the radio's speakers.

"Oh shit. This was the cut back in the day," Ishmael exclaimed, reaching over and turning up the volume.

"The cut? What you know about that, young boy?" Desiree smirked at him.

"Young boy? Ain't nothing young about me, ma," he retorted.

"Yeah, alright. You don't nothing about this song. This was before your time," she said, laughing.

"What? Oh yeah, peep this." He began to sing along with the song.

Desiree was grinning from ear to ear. He actually sounded pretty good, she thought. It was still funny to her, as thuggish as he was that he actually had a soft side. Ishmael grabbed her hand and continued to sing. When the hook came, he waved their arms from side to side, and she joined in on the song.

"Ooh ooh ooh ooh hooo!" They both burst into laughter because she sounded like a coyote howling at the moon.

"Alright, you got that. You need to quit that so-called day job and start pressing records. That's definitely a better career move for you," she teased.

"Well, you definitely need to keep your night job at IHOP," he joked.

She playfully tapped him. The next song that came on was "There'll Never Be" by Switch.

"Oh see now, no they didn't have to take it there. This was my cut." She snapped her fingers, feeling the groove.

"Don't sing, baby. Let me get this one," he continued to tease her.

"Shut up, Ishmael." She laughed.

Ishmael wasn't joking. He liked the song, too, and began to serenade her once again. This time he showed her what he could really do vocally. Desiree was in awe, listening to him belt out the high tone of the lead singer.

Chills ran up her arm while he hypnotized her with his vocals.

Desiree stared at him with melting eyes. He continued to hold her hand and sing. Once the song was over, he kissed the back of her hand with his soft lips. She pulled her hand from his. She was flustered. The way Ishmael made her feel was overwhelming. She didn't think there was another man on earth who could make her feel the way Bilal did. But there was, and his name was Ishmael.

Bilal would roll over in his grave if he knew what she was doing, she thought. She stared out of the window thinking about Bilal and how she missed him so much. She didn't want to lose the love she had for him, but if she continued with Ishmael, that was inevitable. No, she couldn't let that happen, she knew Ishmael was heavy in the game and with that she knew it would be a matter of time before the drama started.

Ishmael saw the change in her behavior. He was somewhat use to her mood swings. He knew all about her secrets from Beverly—or so he thought—but she didn't know he knew. He understood that sometimes your past resurfaces and can change your mood. He, too, had secrets he held within, and sometimes they surfaced, haunting him.

He quickly got on another subject to help clear up whatever was on her mind. He was determined not to let anything ruin this night.

"So have you registered for school yet?" he asked.

"Actually, I did that today." She looked at him, surprised.

"What, you thought I forgot?" He looked over at her.

"Well, yeah, I did."

"I pay attention to you when you talk, Rae," he assured her.

"I see, and I'm impressed."

"No, I'm impressed with you and you furthering your education. I think that's important."

She sat back in the seat and smiled to herself. *This man is something else. He always manages to amaze me.*

They continued to talk about the subjects she registered for in school and what her goals were going to be when she finished.

A half hour later they pulled up in front of the club. The valet rushed to the driver side while another valet opened the door for her. The line was still draped around the corner with people trying to get in. She looked at all the people standing outside and felt a sudden rush of stardom. Everyone gawked at her and Ishmael as if they were the guests of honor. His demeanor portrayed him as some kind of superstar, and he flaunted it as such. He grabbed her hand and led her to the doors.

After the little Italian man gave the sign to let them in, they proceeded in through the doors. Desiree didn't like the fact that they had to be searched. Ishmael saw her expression as the female guard patted her down and searched her purse. He explained to her as they walked toward the elevator the purpose of the security. He didn't let her know that fifty percent of the guests were ballers and that the club was owned by one of the made bosses.

Once inside the elevator, he placed his arm around her waist, pulling her close to him. She looked up into his eyes and inhaled his cologne—Chrome by Azzaro. She loved the smell of it. Their gaze was so intimate that they both began to lean toward each other for a passionate kiss, until the clinking of the elevator distracted them. Two walls opened, and the blare of the music and noise filled the space in the elevator.

Desiree was flabbergasted. She had never been to such an event, and she had been to the most elite corporate affairs, but they couldn't touch the party she and Ishmael had just entered.

There was everything—crap tables, black jack tables, roulette wheels, and pool tables. There were female strippers in one section of the room dancing on a small stage with a pole down the middle and male strippers in another section dancing on a small stage. A glass elevator took guests to an upper level, which had a balcony that wrapped around the entire place. The dance floor was huge and filled with people. The bar wrapped around half the entire lower level. People surrounded every inch of it. There were short round tables with chairs and tall round table with stools. There were sofas and love seats. There were even vending machines with plenty of candy and chips. In another corner, a chef was preparing stir-fried foods and special gourmet. There was a turkey on a rotisserie and a cook carving roast beef.

The place looked like a cruise ship on land with all the luxuries that came with the cruise.

Ishmael escorted her toward the bar.

"What you drinking?" he asked her.

"Nothing just yet," she replied, still looking around.

She watched the half-naked women strut around like it was okay to look like sluts. She watched them grope men and watched the men grope them. She started to feel uneasy and held on to Ishmael's hand a little tighter. He could feel her tense, and he put his arm around her shoulder and pulled her closer. He kissed her cheek, reassuring her that she was safe.

The deejay was pumping the music, and people jumped up and down like they were at a concert.

Derrick appeared out of nowhere with Nate and Dice close behind him. They all gave Ishmael some dap. Ishmael introduced Desiree to the men, and he and Derrick began to converse privately, speaking into each other's ears.

Desiree wanted to go to the ladies' room. She nudged Ishmael, and he leaned over to hear what she had to say.

"Where's the ladies room?" she shouted over the music.

He looked around the room. "It's over there," he said, pointing to the left side of the club. "Hold up. I'm gonna get Nate and Dice to walk you over there."

"Why? I'm a big girl. I can find it myself."

"Oh no doubt, but I don't trust none of these cats up in here. They going with you and that's that." He looked at her. "A'ight?"

"Okay. If you insist," she surrendered, feeling like she was on top of

CHAPTER 20

DOWNTOWN

Sitting at a large round table in the basement of city hall were members of the Drug Enforcement Task Force better known as DETF.

Seated were Robert Cohen, chief of police; Arnold Bowen, assistant to the mayor; Thomas Littleton, director of special units; and David Weston, deputy of operations.

The men were indulging in their usual Saturday night endeavor of poker. Smoke filled the room and bottles of beer and Johnny Walker sat on the table.

"In your face," Cohen yelled as he threw down his hand, displaying a straight flush.

All threw in their hands as they grunted in defeat—except Thomas who was still holding his hand with a smile spreading across his thin, pale lips.

"Read 'em and weep, buddy." Thomas laid the cards on the table, revealing a royal flush.

"Fuck," Cohen yelled and smacked the table. This was the first hand he had lost all night. He was still the big winner so far—he hated to lose at anything. He was a challenger whether on the streets or at poker. One hand lost meant defeat for him, even if he walked away with all the money, which he did almost every Saturday night.

The room erupted with laughter. The men began to refill their glasses and popped the tops to bottled beer. Some lit cigarettes or cigars as they prepared for the next hand. Thomas pulled the pile of money toward him and began to count it. Cohen eyed him with envy although he had a stack of bills sitting in front of him larger then anyone's in the room.

Cohen was your average redneck with the attitude to match. His skin was red, and he was overweight with a protruding belly.

"So what are we going to do with that punk Ish-mail?" Weston asked.

"I'm still waiting to hear word from Leroy," Bowen responded.

"Waiting?" Weston inquired, confused.

"We don't wait for no one. What the hell kind of shit is that?" Cohen yelled.

"Hold on, Cohen," Bowen interrupted. "Give the man some time to set things up."

Cohen barked out loud with laughter, "That nigger has to follow the rules just like every other jigga-boo out there. He's not exempt from the rules. I'll shut that tar baby down."

Weston and Littleton agreed with a nod. Bowen continued to shuffle the cards, clearly showing signs of agitation.

"I told you he'll come through," Bowen said through clenched teeth. "That kid brings in a lot of money from this city. Don't go jumping the gun and fuck this up for all of us."

Cohen let out another laugh. "Hey, Arnie boy, don't get your shorts in a ruffle. I know you feel connected to these people and all, but this is business, and you know it. We've been doing this for many years, and nothing has changed about the way we get a piece of the pie to protect these street scum. Now I know you feel some kind of closeness with them at times because of...you know...you being half monkey and all," he sarcastically teased.

Weston and Littleton bellowed out with laughter. Littleton spit out beer onto the floor and continued to roar.

"I'm not half nigger!" Bowen yelled, furious. "I told you that my great-grandmother was half black because her mother was raped. My skin is as white as yours. The reason being my family stuck with the white color line. I don't have an ounce of nigger blood in me."

His skin became flush red. He hated to be reminded of his family's past. Truth of the matter was his great, great, great-grandmother was black. She was a slave and was raped by the slave master, therefore creating his great, great-grandmother whose skin was very light. She grew up to bare children by a white man, so the light skin got lighter with each generation.

He despised black people. He tolerated them when it was business and there was money to be made. He was picked on as a child whenever someone from his mother's side of the family came to visit, because they were light-skinned blacks. Bowen was as white as they came, but the one thing that he could not escape from his African American heritage was his full lips.

All through grammar school all the way up through college he would come in contact with some kind of pressure from his peers about his background. A Harvard graduate, he vowed that every chance he got, he would stick it to a nigger.

"Hold on now there, Arnie. Bobby is right. What makes this punk so special that he gets a timeline? You know the rules: either he plays or he pays, simple as that," Littleton interjected.

"I know all about the rules," Bowen said as he dealt out the next hand. "The mayor wants to give Leroy a chance to talk to him. Now what are we gonna do? Go against the mayor and the governor?" He looked in each of their faces.

"Bullshit!" Cohen retorted as he scooped up his cards and studied them. "That niggers got over half the city in the palm of his hands. Now you and I both know that's too much power for one nigger to have. You tell the mayor to talk to that old nigger and tell him he's got thirty days to come back with an answer on that punk or I'm going all out, and I don't give a fuck what happens after that."

The men continued to play poker, laughing and talking. Once the hand was over, Bowen excused himself.

"I gotta go to the can." He got up and left the room.

Once inside of the bathroom he stood in front of the urinal and re-lieved himself. He rocked back and forth, clearly showing his consumption of alcohol. Once he was done, he pulled the phone from his waist and began to dial.

"Hello."

"It's me Arnie."

"What is it, Arnie? I'm out of town with my wife," the mayor said.

"I'm playing poker with the guys."

"Yeah? Who's winning?"

"Cohen is, as usual. I swear I think that fat fuck cheats."

"Arnie, I'm sure you didn't call me to talk about the poker game. What's on your mind?"

"Cohen's putting pressure on me, Tony. He wants an answer from Leroy in thirty days, or he's going to unleash the dogs. You know we can't have that type of publicity so close to election time."

"Fuck!" the mayor shouted. He blew out a deep breath into the phone. "Who does that fat bastard think he is?"

"I know, sir, but you know he'll do it. That wouldn't look good for you, Tony."

"Yeah, I know. What do the other guys say about it?"

"They agree with him. You know they have their heads so far up his ass they taste shit every morning when they wake up," Bowen said, pacing the floor. There was silence.   "Tony, are you there?"

"All right. I'll get in touch with Leroy and get back to you. One day somebody's going to give that fat fucker Cohen just what he needs," the mayor spat.

"I agree, sir, but until then, you need to uphold your image. So for now we play by the jerk's rules until after you're re-elected then you can stick it to his lard ass."

"You're right, Arnie. Okay then, it's settled. I'll talk to you later."

Bowen replaced his phone in the case and looked at his reflection in the dingy mirror. He brushed his hand over his short-cropped hair and walked out of the bathroom without washing his hands.

CHAPTER 21

PARTNERS IN CRIME

Zola walked into the house and headed straight for the bedroom. She was vexed. She found out about the industry party through Damon. She wanted to go, but Ishmael wouldn't tell her where the party was. She had called Damon and told him what Ishmael said and that she was going to crash the party anyway. He told her not to worry, he would keep an eye on him, but he thought it was best for her not to show up either. Damon also wouldn't disclose the location of the party. Truth be told, Damon wanted to get his groove on without any hassles. Zola would definitely be a problem if she came to the party.

She walked into the closet, reaching up and pulling the chain to turn on the ceiling light. She pulled the lever that protruded from the wall and removed the panel. The shelf behind the wall that was mounted over the safe was bare.

"Shit," she exclaimed.

She played around with the dials on the safe, which only frustrated her more. She tried birthday combinations, telephone numbers, and nothing worked. She plopped down in the middle of the floor and sat pouting.

Ishmael's scent lingered in the closet like a rain cloud in the sky. She had never seen him do anything violent, but the rumors and his creditability on the streets were proof enough for anyone. And that's what attracted her to him in the first place: his rep on the streets—and of course the mountains of paper he held didn't hurt either.

Her cell phone began to ring. She ran to her purse and retrieved it. "Hello."

"What's up, girl?" It was Zola's shysty partner Nettie.

Nettie and Zola had been best friends since they where kids.

Nettie was a stripper and one of the most sinister bitches on the planet. She was nice with a razor, and she always had one tucked away safely in her mouth. She'd been that way for years and had the rep of slicing a nigga with a quickness. Had it not been for Zola, Nettie would've got at Ishmael a long time ago. She despised him, and he didn't hide his feelings for her either. Both put up with each other on the strength of Zola. Although Nettie had helped Zola with her devious ways on plenty of occasions, Zola would not allow Nettie to take away the butter that coated her bread.

"What you getting into?" Zola inquired.

"What makes you think I'm getting into something?" Nettie asked defensively.

"Because, when aren't you into something," Zola shot back.

"Oh, a bitch got jokes, huh?"

"Aw, don't be like that. You so sensitive," Zola teased.

"No, that trick you living with is sensitive, with his punk ass."

"Oh, don't do it like that. That ain't even right."

"I ain't call you for this. You want to hang out with me, or are you on lock down?" Nettie cracked.

"Picture that shit. Just bring your ass over, and we'll think about what to get into when you get here."

Twenty minutes later Nettie walked through the front door. She looked Zola up and down as she walked past her.

"What?" Zola inquired.

Nettie continued to walk toward the sofa and plopped down onto it.

"What's your problem?"

"Nothing. Where's yo' buster at?"

"He went out. You ain't dancing tonight?"

"Naw, I'm off. So what's up? What you tryna do t'night?" Nettie asked as she retrieved a blunt from her purse.

"I wanted to crash the industry party everybody went to tonight, but I think I'll pass on that." Zola sat next to her.

"Let's go by Gerry's," Nettie said, lighting the blunt.

Gerry's was a small neighborhood bar the locals hung out at.

"I ain't tryna go up in there with them bums." Zola turned up her nose. "Them yo' kinda people, not mine."

"Zola, yo' shit stink just like everybody else's." Nettie rolled her eyes.

They sat there in silence, passing the blunt back and forth.

"Fuck it. Let's go round there and see what's up," Zola said, getting off the sofa.

They rode in Zola's Range Rover. They approached the club and saw several people posted out front.

"See what I'm sayin'? Look at these bums out here." Zola pointed.

"How you figure they bums, Zo?" Nettie looked over at her.

"Look at how they dressed. No style whatsoever. Them niggaz ain't holdin' no paper." She continued to drive past the bar.

"Zo, don't let the gear fool you. Please believe me. Some of them niggas is holding big time."

"Nettie, I ain't feeling that place."

"Come on, Zo. Let's just go in for a minute, then we can leave and go wherever you want to go."

Zola sucked her teeth and busted a U-turn and found a park under a streetlight at the corner. The women strolled across the street, heading toward the club. A black E320 Benz with black tinted windows crept up the street behind them. Once the car was parallel to the women, the driver side window lowered halfway, revealing the top part of the driver's face. The driver honked the horn. They both looked in the direction of the vehicle. The driver lowered the window completely, exposing his face.

"What up, Zo?" he shouted.

Zola and Nettie stopped and looked. Zola stared at the car, trying to figure out who the driver was. Then it hit her, so she began to walk over toward the car.

"What's up, lady?" He smiled as he looked her up and down.

She was sporting a pair of Seven Capri jeans that fit like a glove. She had on a pair of Chanel high-heel sandals and a Chanel fitted tank top. She rotated her thick hips as she approached the vehicle.

"Nick D, what's going on?" She returned the smile.

"You, baby. I know you ain't about to go up in that rat trap," he said, referring to the local bar. "That ain't yo' style, ma."

Nick D was a handsome half-black, half Puerto Rican. He had status from several towns over. He was well known and got along pretty much with all the other dealers. He was a stand-up type of dude—until you pushed him. He never put in his own work because he had his own personal goon squad for that. They weren't big time but they were known.

"I'm here with Nettie. She be sweating these knuckleheads, not me," she defended.

"Oh, that's Nettie?" he said, surprised. "I ain't seen her ass in a minute. What up, Nettie Nett?" he yelled.

"Who dat?" Nettie yelled back from across the street.

"Come see," Zola responded.

Nettie strolled across the street toward the Benz.

"Oh shit. What's good, Nick?" She smiled.

"You, ma. Where you been hidin'?"

"Nowhere, man. I be around. What you doing around here?"

"Just cruising," he replied nonchalantly.

"Yeah, a'ight. You know you out here cunt hunting." She laughed.

"Naw, man, these chicken heads ain't about shit out here." He smiled. "Yo, you still sucking on that blade?"

Nettie rolled her tongue around in her mouth and flicked it out, exposing the blade on it then she flipped it back in her mouth and tucked it away.

"Damn! I can't believe you still sucking on that blade. You gonna fuck around and get gangrene on your tongue, and they gonna have to cut that motherfucker off." He laughed.

Zola agreed with him as she, too, laughed.

"Keep talking, slick nigga, and you can get it too," she retorted.

"Hold up, ma. I'm on your side," he surrendered. "I know you nice with that silver so pump your brakes. I'm just fucking with you."

Nettie noticed someone she knew and walked off up the street.

"So what's good, ma?" Nick inquired.

"Nothing much."

"So you still swinging with that cat Ish?"

"Yeah, something like that." She rolled her eyes.

"He ain't good enough for you, ma. You need to be hanging with a real nigga." He smiled.

"So I guess you would be that nigga, huh?"

"Word up," he bragged.

Zola smiled at the sound of that as she ran her hand along the roof of his car, admiring its shine.

"So, what's up?" he asked.

"I ain't messing with Ishmael like that, Nick. That's all I need for him to find out I'm creeping on him."

"Come on, ma. You don't want to be with that cat, and you know it. Come on get in. Let's take a ride."

"I can't do that. Plus, I'm here with Nettie."

"Nett can hold her own. Come on," he edged on.

Zola stared into his handsome face and thought about it. It did sound like a good idea. He was fine as hell, and he was holding paper too.

"Hold up a minute. Let me holler at Nettie for a minute," she said.

Zola pranced toward the club and approached Nettie who was talking with some dude.

"Nett, let me holler at you for a minute," Zola said, interrupting their conversation.

They walked a few feet away from the crowd that had gathered in front of the bar's entrance.

"What's up?" Nettie inquired.

"I'm gonna roll with Nick."

"What? Roll where?" Nettie eyed her.

"We gonna get something to eat."

"And how am I supposed to get back to your house and get my car? You just gonna leave me here?"

"Aw, Nettie, don't front. You know you wanna stay here," Zola said. "Here take my keys and drive the Rover back to the house and leave the keys in the mailbox." She held the keys out for Nettie to take.

"You act like you ain't coming home for the night."

"I'm coming home. I'm just getting something to eat."

"Yeah, okay. So what's up with that?" Nettie asked with an attitude.

"Ain't nothing up but what I just said. I'm going to get something to eat." Zola turned and sashayed away.

"Ho," Nettie called out after her.

CHAPTER 22

LET ME FIND OUT

They arrived in front of the Copa. Ishmael pulled into a parking spot. Partygoers flocked the entrance. Latinos, Dominicans, and Puerto Ricans were rushing in through the front doors.

Desiree looked around at the scene in confusion. The outside of the club resembled a castle. Once inside, the many lights sparkled all around. The atmosphere was bright and energetic.

Ishmael held Desiree's hand and lead her to a table. The music was fast and loud. The cymbals and conga drums were the loudest of the many instruments that the band played. There were couples on the floor twirling and spinning around.

Desiree was dizzy just watching them twirl. A waitress walked around with a tray of tropical drinks held high above her head. Different types of fruit descended from the tall glasses. Ishmael saw Desiree eyeing the mouthwatering drinks.

"Would you like a drink?"

"Yes, that would be nice." She smiled.

As the waitress floated by with the now-empty tray, Ishmael grabbed her hand.

"Yes." She smiled. The waitress was a Latino beauty. She had long, jet-black wavy hair that fell well below her shoulders. She had freshly tanned skin and a voluptuous sexy body.

"Can you bring us a Bahama Mama and a Grand Marnier?"

The pretty woman smiled and nodded as she sashayed away to fetch the drinks.

"What is this place?" Desiree asked, looking around.

"Oh, this used to be a favorite spot of mine."

"A favorite spot?" Desiree looked at him, confused.

"Yeah." He smiled at her. "Why?"

"Because this doesn't seem like your style."

"Oh yeah? What's my style?'

"Well…you know?"

"No, I don't know. That's why I'm asking." He stared deep into her eyes.

"Well...like the place we just came from. That seems more like your style."

The waitress returned with their drinks. They took them and toasted each other. Desiree sipped her drink, and the fruity passion slid down the back of her throat.

They sat and drank their drinks and enjoyed the scenery while engrossing in deep conversation.

Suddenly the band began to play "Lloraras" by Oscar D'Leon.

"Come on." Ishmael grabbed her hand, pulling her to her feet, practically dragging Desiree to the floor.

She was nervous. She knew nothing about dancing the salsa.

Once on the dance floor Ishmael pulled her close. They were face to face. He held her around her waist and held her right hand. They stood there eye to eye for a few seconds. He swayed her side to side, slowly at first.

"Ishmael, I don't know how to do this," she said.

"Don't worry. I got you. Just loosen your body and relax. Let me lead you, and you move with me." He smiled.

She nodded.

Ishmael picked up the pace, swaying side to side, never taking his eyes off hers. They began to turn around slowly at first.

"Just listen to the beat. Let the music carry you away," he instructed.

Desiree didn't know what that meant, but she gave it a try. She closed her eyes and tried to concentrate. Ishmael got into the grove of the music and took Desiree on a ride like no other. His pelvis moved from side to side against hers. She could feel his bulge pressing against her. They glided on the floor like they were on skates.

Desiree couldn't believe she was doing the salsa. She had never thought in a million years she would even have the opportunity to, let alone actually dance it. She opened her eyes, and Ishmael was still staring deeply at her. His intensity made moisture seep from her treasures. She became nervous again and began to move off beat and stepped on Ishmael's feet continuously.

"Okay, that's enough," he said. "I'ma have all kinds of corns and bunions and shit by the time you finish with my feet." He laughed.

They were on their way back to New Jersey. Desiree stared out the window, basking in her thoughts. She had a slight smile on her face as she gazed.

Ishmael looked over at her. "What you thinking about?"

"Oh nothing," she said, breaking out of her gaze.

"Come on now. I can see it all over your face."

"Well," she said as she adjusted herself in the seat, "I was thinking about how I wish you were a different man."

"Why?"

"Because you sell drugs, Ishmael."

"Why are you so against it, Rae? It's not like you've always lived your life like Mother Theresa."

She looked at him with confused eyes. "How do you know how I lived?"

"I don't," he lied, avoiding eye contact.

She looked away. "My old life is in the past, and I'd like to keep it there."

Ishmael didn't press the issue.

They pulled up in front of Beverly's house. It was 4:30 A.M. He turned off the ignition and laid his head back on the seat.

"Ishmael, I really enjoyed myself tonight. Thank you."

"It's all good," he said, looking over at her.

They sat and talked for about half an hour.

"It's late, so I'm going to go on in the house."

They exited the car and walked up the steps onto the porch. The night air was still and warm. Desiree turned to him and stepped forward. He grabbed her around the waist, and they engaged in a deep kiss. The passion was breathtaking, causing her to release juices again. She broke their embrace and opened the door.

"Thank you again," she said, not looking at him, and walked into the hallway.

"I'll call you," he said.

On the drive home, Ishmael thought about her. It bugged the hell out of him where he'd seen her before. It was her eyes. It was something about them that had him thinking they were familiar. There was something else she was keeping from him besides the robbery and her doing time. He was definitely feeling Desiree, and he was gonna make it happen with her one way or another.

CHAPTER 23

RIDIN HIGH

Desiree was sitting on the front porch reading *Sincerely Yours* by Al-Saadiq Banks. She was so engrossed in the novel that she blocked everything out around her. Children played loudly in the streets. Music blared from passing cars. She was so intrigued by the author's style that she imagined herself as one of the characters.

Suddenly a motorcycle raced up the street, interrupting her reading. It zoomed back and forth past the house at high speeds. From one end of the block, back and forth it went. She watched as the man on the bike raced past her. His physique was phenomenal. His muscular arms were exposed and covered with tattoos. The way the rider leaned forward on the bike as he handled the monster turned her on. She desperately wondered what the secret cyclist looked like without his helmet.

The children in the street watched him in amazement as he zoomed past them again. There was an outburst of *ooh*s and *ahh*s. Desiree stood, looking toward the corner where several men were standing to see what was going on. The cyclist was coming up the street at a high speed with the front wheel high in the air. As he past, Desiree admired the muscles in his arms, flexing as he showed their strength while holding the front wheel in place. The children jumped up and down, applauding the man and his circus act. Desiree felt goose bumps invade her arms. She was totally turned on and imagined herself on the back of the bike holding the man around his waist tightly.

The cyclist continued with the wheelie all the way to the end of the next block with an audience watching until he placed the front wheel to the ground. She watched as the cycle made a U-turn and headed back toward her. She didn't want the man to see that she was still watching so she sat back down and planted her head into the book, anxiously waiting for him to drive past again so that she could sneak a peek.

The motorcycle cruised down the street slowly as it came to a full stop in front of the house. She raised her head in confusion. She became nervous as the man pulled the bike to the curb and shut off the ignition.

Who is this? she thought.

The man began to remove the helmet. Desiree's heart was beating fast and hard. She would finally get to see who the mystery man was behind the helmet.

He pulled the helmet up slowly, and his face was revealed. It was Ishmael. He was sporting a black bandana on his head. He smiled brightly at her. Her heart raced around in her body like an Indy 500 racecar. She jumped to her feet and ran down the steps and embraced him tightly.

"Show off." She smiled at him.

"All for you, baby." He smiled and placed a succulent kiss on her lips.

"Whose bike is this?"

"It's mine." He smiled, kissing her again.

The children on the block crowded around the bike. They began to ask Ishmael tons of questions about it. Several asked for a ride.

"Not now, fellas. Maybe later, a'ight?" he said.

They looked disappointed with his answer. An ice cream truck turned the corner onto the block. Ishmael reached in his pocket and pulled out a ten-dollar bill and handed it to the oldest of the children.

"Here. Y'all go get some ice cream."

"Yea," they all screamed.

"Hey. Make sure you get them all an ice cream or you won't get a ride on the bike," he said to the boy with the money.

The kids took off running up the street.

"How sweet was that?" Desiree admired his kindness.

"Ay, you know how I do it. I love the kids. Actually I'm sorta practicing for when I finally have my own." He gave her a mischievous look.

"Oh yeah?"

"Yeah," he said, grabbing hold of her waist and pulling her close.

They were face to face, and Desiree could feel the warm air that came from his nose. He kissed her forehead lightly.

"You wanna go for a ride?"

"I don't know, Ish," she said, hesitating.

She wanted nothing more in the world than to ride on the back of his bike holding on to him for dear life, but she was afraid of bikes. All the deaths they caused were not what she wanted to experience.

After a few short moments of trying to convince her to go for a ride, Ishmael gave up. They sat on the porch and talked for a while. Ishmael received a call on his cell phone that seemed to be urgent. He kissed her on the cheek and hurried off on his bike, speeding up the street.

She watched him pull off. She was curious as to who he spoke to on the phone to cause him to rush off.

A man walked by and clearly by the way he walked he was high off heroin. He would take a few steps then stop, scratch himself, and then go into a nod. This behavior reminded her of Bilal.

CHAPTER 24

EXCUSE MY BACK

"Damn, Leroy, what was so important that you couldn't tell me over the phone?" Ishmael inquired.

"Youngun, you know the damn rules. No conversation about business over the airwaves."

"A'ight. So what's up?"

"What are you going to do about my proposition?" Leroy was serious.

Ishmael thought again about if he really wanted to make a deal with the devil to be protected by dirty cops. He thought about if he agreed to their terms then there would be other shit that the crooked cops would start asking for.

"I don't know, man. I think I'm gonna pass."

"Sit down, son."

They were in the office of the local pool hall that Leroy owned. It wasn't your typical office environment. The office was tricked out with a fireplace that had a bear-skin rug sitting in front of it. The walls were covered with paintings of naked supermodels. The furniture was European, flown in on a special shipment.

Ishmael took a seat in one of the European leather chairs. A blond-haired, blue-eyed beauty handed him a glass of Cognac. He looked up at her, and her mountains of cleavage stared down at him. He shifted his eyes toward Leroy. The blond beauty smiled and glided off out of the room, leaving the men alone.

"I got a lot of heat coming down on me from the top about your position in this city. Ishmael, I wouldn't come to you about this unless it was something of importance. I knew your father when he was the slickest pimp there was. He had a stable of the baddest bitches miles deep."

Ishmael shifted in his chair, uneasiness showing on his face. He had heard this story a million times. He'd seen the pictures of his father and the many different women he'd had—his mother being his bottom bitch. Ishmael hated his father and did not idolize him one bit. He had his mother on the stroll and turned her out on heroin. Ishmael was dropped off with the one woman he had always known to take care of him: his grandmother.

He knew who his mother was and always longed to be with her, but his father saw to it that that never happened. His father didn't even acknowledge Ishmael as his own. Once his mother lost her sex appeal and beauty due to the abuse from using dope, his father kicked her out of his stable, leaving her penniless and a hardcore main liner. His mother returned to his grandmother, seeking shelter only to die of an overdose one month later.

When his mother came home, Ishmael was happy to finally be with her. He dreamed of the day she would come home, and when she did, she was gone just like that, leaving him heart broken all over again. Ishmael was nine years old when she died. He would hear his grandmother cry about his father killing his mother. She talked about it with her friends constantly.

Knowing his mother died from an overdose of heroin, he contemplated on many occasions avoiding selling dope and straight dealing with cocaine. But Ishmael was a hustler and loved to chase paper, and the major part of his flow came from heroin.

He definitely had no love for his father, and when his father was found dead in an alleyway, he was all too happy to put the man who killed his mother out of his mind. His father was found shot fifteen times sitting in his brand-new Cadillac Sedan Deville.

Leroy talked and talked about his father while Ishmael zoned out and thought about Desiree.

"So, you see, that's why you need to take my advice. If you don't, youngun, them mafuckas are gon' to make it hard for you."

"Who's gonna make it hard for me?" he asked.

Leroy shook his head. "Where was your head at when I was talking to you?"

"OG, listen. I got too much going on right now to be pressed about some square-ass downtown cats."

"Those are powerful men. Let me tell you something: You young punks don't last too long in this business because you got your nuts rammed up some fish-smelling bitch's pussy. Get your head right, boy, and be smart." Leroy stood.

Ishmael stared into the old man's eyes. He felt his wrath and knew from where he was coming. All the game in the world wasn't enough to compare to the pull Leroy had. Ishmael respected him to the fullest—after all he put him down on the game. He took him under his wing and treated him like his own son.

"A'ight, so what I gotta do?" Ishmael asked, still staring stone faced at Leroy.

Leroy took a seat and reached into an antique wooden box that sat on his desk. He took out one of his Cuban cigars and lit it, taking deep puffs.

"You report to me and me only. I'll be your connect, and you're to only purchase from me. At the end of every week you bring me forty-five percent of the money you pull in, whether you get rid of the weight or not." He sat back and rocked in his chair.

"Forty-five percent? That shit is crazy."

"It is what it is, youngun." Leroy shrugged.

"I got my own connect now and the weight and quality is on point," Ishmael reasoned.

"It don't matter who you cop from, son, because whoever it is, I'm sure they cop from my people," Leroy said with confidence.

"Why the fuck do I have to give you forty-five percent?"

"You ain't giving me forty-five percent, Ishmael. I get ten percent to keep the deal, then I throw the other thirty-five percent to those cocksuckers downtown." He laughed.

"Why can't those bums come to me for a straight deal? You profit off me as the middle man."

"You don't hold no weight downtown, Ishmael. Don't look at it as a profit. Look at it as an investment."

"Investment? Investment for who? You?" Ishmael inquired.

"No, for you, youngun. With me keeping the feds off your ass keeps you worry free, and with you being worry free, you run your operation with a level head. I keep the heat off you and the temperature at a comfortable degree. You dig?" Leroy schooled.

"You killing me, Roy."

"Hey, son, who said shit in life was free."

"Man, fuck that. I don't need them mafuckas to protect me. I got my own security," Ishmael retorted.

Leroy leaned forward on his forearms. "You don't want to fuck with them."

"You know I never thought I'd see the day you'd bow down to no man," Ishmael said, shaking his head in disappointment. "I used to idolize you. I looked up to you. I loved you more than I did my own father—and I hated his black-hearted ass."

"What do you want from me, Ishmael? They got us all by the nuts. It's either play the game their way or get played. I could go to war because I damn sure got the muscle, but I'm too old, and frankly, I don't care to. And how long do you think you gonna last going up against the politician, police force, and government? Not long." He shook his head, showing clear hurt over Ishmael's actions.

"Fuck that. No deal. I don't bow down to nobody. Ishmael stands on his own." He patted his chest. "You can stay on your knees and suck dick if you want to but frankly I prefer sucking pussy," Ishmael said, standing.

Leroy sat back in his chair, staring at him. "That's a bad move on your part, Ishmael, a bad move."

There was silence in the room as the two men stared each other down, neither of them blinking.

"So that's your decision?" Leroy asked.

"Fuck yeah," Ishmael stated calm and cool.

"When the shit hits the fan, I can't help you, so don't come to me." Leroy turned his high-back leather chair around so that his back was facing Ishmael.

"So it's like that, Leroy? You turning your back on me? You was like a father to me and you gon' turn your back on your son?"

Leroy didn't say a word. All that could be seen was the clouds of smoke from his cigar streaming into the air.

Ishmael thought about how if the OG's that since died knew Leroy was siding with the system, breaking the code of the streets, they would turn over in their graves.

Ishmael walked out of the room with distress and pain written all over his face. This man took him under his wing and did things for him his own father didn't do. Leroy was like the father he never had.

CHAPTER 25

THE TIME HAS COME

Desiree had just gotten off the bus after going to check out an apartment a coworker had told her about. She switched the heavy book bag to her other shoulder and began the several-block walk home. School was going great, but working the hours she did and going to school was a little hard.

When she walked into the apartment she was relieved to see Beverly and the kids weren't home.

Beverly had found her a boyfriend, and she had been staying away from home a lot. He was an older man who lived across town. He was a drinker like Beverly, but the difference between the two was he was a hardworking man. He drove a pickup truck, and he would come pick up Beverly, and the kids would pile in the back of the truck.

Desiree showered and made her something to eat. After eating, she sat down at the kitchen table to do her homework. She had a few hours to spare before she would go to bed to get a quick nap before work.

Her assignment was to plan a financial budget for a business owner whose business was losing money. She needed to create the formula that would stabilize and allow the business to profit.

She opened her book to the page that was assigned to her group. The owner of the business listed all revenue and expenses. Desiree stared at the book in shock when she read that the type of business was a bowling alley.

It was Wednesday morning, the day they were going to rob Groovers I. Bilal opened his eyes to a brightly lit room. The sunrays bounced around on his face. He got up and walked over to the window, peering down onto the street. He saw one of the local drug runners standing down on the sidewalk below the window. He opened the window and stuck his head out.

"Beaver," he yelled.

The young man looked up toward the window.

"Wassup?"

"What time is it, man?" Bilal asked.

"What I look like to you? A clock?" Beaver said sarcastically.

"Just tell me what time it is, youngun."

The young man looked at his watch.

"It's 9:07. You need to buy you a damn watch instead of a bag of dope."

Bilal closed the window and walked over to the mattress.

"Rae-Rae, get up."

Desiree moaned and pulled the covers over her face.

"Rae-Rae, we need to talk. I don't think the time is right," he said as he sat down on the mattress.

Desiree threw the covers off her face. "You don't think the time is right? How long we gotta wait, Bunchy? Listen, it's now or never, babe. I'm ready to get this paper."

"Yeah, but Rae-Rae, do you realize if we get caught that we could do some hard time?"

"Bunchy, stop being a punk. This plan is perfect. There is no way we can get caught. You said so yourself." She got up and walked into the bathroom.

Bilal lay back on the mattress and folded his arms across his forehead.

Bilal walked into the restaurant. There were two men sitting at the counter and three women seated at one of the tables. The waitress had just finished taking their orders. She brushed past him as he approached the counter and sat down on one of the stools.

"Hey, suga, you want something to eat?" she asked him.

"Naw, I'm okay. Can you tell Rae-Rae to come out here for me?"

"Well what's the matter? You look so down and out."

"I'm good," he stated wearily.

"Okay. If you say so."

The waitress disappeared behind the swinging doors. After a few moments, Desiree appeared.

"What's up, babe?"

"Where is the bag, Rae-Rae?"

"It's in my locker in the locker room."

"I need it."

"For what, Bunchy?"

"Rae-Rae, please not now. Just get me the bag."

"Bunchy, you're going to fuck this up. What's wrong with you? Stop trippin," she whispered.

"I'm not trippin, Rae-Rae. Forget it."

He stormed out of the restaurant heading for the stairs leading up to the offices. Desiree watched him with concerned eyes.

"I hope he don't mess this up," she said to herself.

Bilal was outside in the back of the bowling alley taking a smoke break, deep in thought as he leaned against the building. Desiree came outside and approached him.

"Are you all right?"

"I guess so," he said solemnly.

"Listen, baby, we're in this together. After we do this, we can leave town and go somewhere and settle down. Live a new life," she said, trying to cheer him up.

"A new life, Rae-Rae? How we gonna live a new life? We addicts. There ain't no new life for a addict. All addicts' lives are the same wherever you go."

"No, Bunchy, we can get a new flat—hell we can get a house with the kind of money we gonna get. We could buy nice things for ourselves, travel, and have a good time."

"Yeah," he said, shaking his head.

They both walked back into the bowling alley. Desiree headed for the kitchen while Bilal looked up at the bowling alley's clock. It was

12:45 P.M. *He walked over to the front door and looked around the parking lot. His heart was beating harder in his chest than usual. He thought about the plan over and over in his head. His stomach began to quiver. He needed a hit.*

Bilal went into the men's room. Once inside, he looked in each stall to make sure no one was there. He went into a stall, closing it and locking it. He sat down on the toilet and retrieved the tiny baggy from his cigarette pack. He took a book of matches out of his shirt pocket and bent the corners, then he dipped the bent matchbook corner into the off-white substance. Scooping a nice-size portion out of the bag, he brought it to his nostril and sniffed. He did this twice in each nostril and put away his product. He walked over to the mirror and checked the contents of his nose to make sure no residue was showing. He looked at himself in the mirror and waited for the drug to take effect as he felt the drainage from the dope slide from his nose down the back of his throat. He glided out of the bathroom and proceeded back to the office located next to Harry's huge office.

He moved a picture of Super-Fly that hung on the wall. Behind the picture was a perfectly drilled hole looking right into Harry's office. He peeked into the hole and saw Harry sitting at his desk talking on the phone while his assistant gave him head.

It was getting close to four o'clock when the money would be delivered. Bilal walked over to two more pictures and checked the drilled holes in the wall. After everything looked to be in order, he walked over to the huge steam pipe that came from the ceiling leading to the floor. He squeezed his skinny hand behind the pipe and felt for the towel he'd placed there, pulling it out. He unraveled the towel, exposing two .32 caliber weapons.

"Now or never, baby," he heard Desiree's voice say in his head.

CHAPTER 26

PRIDE

Desiree was standing out front of IHOP waiting for Ishmael to pick her up. She was exhausted. School and work had taken their toll on her, and the fact that this was her second week of not smoking was starting to get to her. But she was determined to stay smoke free of the cancer sticks and to keep the deal she and Ishmael had. He agreed to stop eating the violet candy if she agreed to give up cigarettes. But he still had one up on her because since he quit eating the candy he smoked weed more. But that didn't bother her because weed was never her drug of choice—when she tried it, it made her paranoid.

She walked over and sat on a bench—her feet were killing her. She began to think about Bilal as she spotted Ishmael pulling into the parking lot, and the thought left her mind just as quick as it came.

She jumped into the truck, and they sped off. Neither of them uttered a word. Ishmael was in his own thoughts, and Desiree was just plain ole tired. Minutes later she looked over at him. She could see something was bothering him. In fact, for the last several weeks, he had seemed to be off in a distance. When they were together she could tell he was trying hard not to show what was obvious to the naked eye. Something was going on, and Desiree could see the hurt in his eyes. The eyes never lie.

"You want to talk about it?" she asked, rubbing his arm.

"I'm good, baby." He gave a weak smile.

Although he was clearly stressing about something Desiree was growing deeper and deeper in love with him. She wanted on so many occasions to make love to him, but her heart wouldn't allow her to do it. She still loved Bilal, although her heart was changing, the more time she spent with Ishmael.

Ishmael looked over at her. She had laid her head back and closed her eyes. He could see how tired she was. He admired her ambition. She was a hardworking woman. She went to school by day and worked at night. She didn't deserve to have to struggle the way she did. But what could he do? She would not allow him to spend a dime outside of dinner and dancing on her. Any gifts he tried to give her she'd give back. Any money he tried to slide to her, she'd refuse.

It often made him feel less than a man that she wouldn't let him take care of her. They were definitely an item, and his boys often ragged on him, saying he didn't have what it took to take care of a woman. But he never let them know what the real deal was.

Zola had been making herself invisible more and more lately. Ishmael had been so wrapped up with Desiree and getting ready for war that he hadn't noticed. All he knew was that it was peaceful at home and the bitching had stopped.

Once he pulled up in front of Beverly's crib he shook Desiree lightly to awaken her.

"Rae, why don't you let me help you?"

"Ishmael, we've been through this before. I don't need any help. I need to do this for myself," she said, wiping her eyes.

"The least you can do is let me get you your own crib."

She sighed out loud and laid her head back onto the headrest. She was exhausted, and she was a little tired of not being able to get any sleep. She had been apartment hunting and didn't have enough money to take any of the apartments she had seen. She was so tired of all the noise that the building and neighborhood kids kept up, causing her to lose hours of sleep. She thought about taking Ishmael up on his offer to help her get a place, but she wanted to do it for herself.

She had always taken care of herself with no help from a man, and she was damn sure not going to start. Ishmael offered her gifts all the time, and on several occasions she wanted to take them so badly. For example, she could sure use a cell phone because Bev didn't have a house phone. He offered her a shopping spree as well. As bad as she needed some decent clothes, she couldn't take it. She did the best she could with the money she made. She didn't seem to see a problem with shopping at Easy Pickins and Payless shoes. They offered the same expensive look at a much lower price.

"I don't know, Ish...maybe—"

"Listen, you can't keep going like this," he said, taking her hand and kissing it ever so gently.

"Okay. We'll talk about it later."

"You're off tonight, right?"

"Yes."

"I'll swing by and pick you up at eight."

"I don't know, Ish. I really need to get me some sleep tonight."

"I'll make sure you get your rest. Just be ready when I come."

She leaned over and pecked him softly on the lips before getting out of the truck.

CHAPTER 27

THE MAYORS OFFICE

"Mr. Mayor, there is a Leroy Jones here to see you, sir," the secretary announced over the intercom.

"Thank you, Lois. Send him in."

Leroy appeared through the door and shut it. He shuffled across the shiny hardwood floor with just a hint of gangster lean in his swagger. He gave a head-nod acknowledgement toward Arnold Bowen who was sitting in a chair.

"Tony," he said, leaning in and giving the mayor a handshake.

"Leroy, my man." The mayor stood and shook his hand with a smile. "Have a seat. What are you drinking?"

"Old Grand Dad," Leroy belted.

"Of course. How could I have forgotten?"

He walked over to his cabinet and poured Leroy a drink.

"So, Leroy, I hope you're here to give me some good news on our young thoroughbred Ishmael." The mayor handed him his drink.

Leroy took a sip and set it down on the marble-top desk. He leaned back in his chair and reached into the inside pocket of his suit jacket. Bowen and the mayor sat patiently anticipating an answer from Leroy who pulled a huge cigar from his pocket and ran it under his nose, inhaling the cigar's aroma.

"He didn't take the deal, Tony. He's got other plans."

"Shit," Bowen projected.

The mayor held up a hand to Bowen, instructing him to calm down. Leroy wet the cigar with his tongue before searching for his lighter.

The mayor chuckled. "What do you mean he didn't take the deal, he's got other plans? You told him about the consequences, didn't you?"

"Of course I did," Leroy said calmly as he popped the lighter and held the flame to the end of the cigar.

"Who does that nigger think he is?" Bowen belted out impatiently.

Leroy cocked his head toward Bowen and stared at him with his piercing eyes.

"Nigger?" Leroy inquired while clouds of smoke escaped his mouth. The mayor got out of his chair and walked over to the window and let it up.

"Now, everybody, let's just calm down for a minute. Leroy, Arnie didn't mean what he said. Did you, Arnie?" The mayor turned and looked at him blankly.

Bowen lowered his head. "No, I didn't mean it at all," he said unconvincingly.

Leroy turned his head and continued to puff on his cigar.

"Okay. Let me see if I understand you correctly, Leroy."

"Tony, you heard me correctly. He ain't going for the deal. These young men today have hearts of stone. Nothing scares them. Frankly, I admire the guts they have."

"Guts? Stupidity is more like it. The balls that kid must have. Big blue ones," Bowen interrupted.

Leroy bellowed out a hearty laugh. "Listen, you little ass wipe, that *kid* got more guts in his left nut than you got in your whole body."

"Fellas please," the mayor interrupted. "We got a situation that needs some attention. All hell is going to break loose if we don't fix this problem before it starts. It's election time, fellas, not to mention the governor is going to shit bricks if he finds out."

"Well, Tony, the way I see it, it's your problem now. I tried. It's a done deal for me," he said, standing. "Oh yeah make sure them cock suckers understand not to fuck with me or mine," Leroy warned.

"Come on, Leroy. Give me a hand here. You know how to talk these people's language. Don't leave me hanging," he pleaded.

"These people's language?" Leroy began to laugh. "You son of a bitch. When was the last time you looked in the mirror? Just 'cause your skin is light don't make you white." Leroy continued to laugh as he shuffled out of the office.

"Fucking niggers," Bowen announced, jumping to his feet.

"Hold on now there, Arnie. Watch your mouth," the mayor warned.

"Oh, come on, Tony. Don't tell me you gonna let that jackass pull that black pride shit over your eyes? You're better then that. Fuck that back-to-Africa, power-to-the-people shit."

The mayor sat in thought. He knew what was about to go down, and his career could be along with it. The governor had given him strict orders to handle this situation or it would be his head. The governor had people to answer to, and he had to answer to the governor. Bowen was an asshole, but he kept him around because of his smarts and loyalty. Although he was a light-skinned black who could pass for white as well, he didn't hate black people the way Bowen did. They both had a lot in common, and they worked well together. Bowen was a hardworking man and brought a lot of political know-how to the team. Bowen did all the mayor's dirty work and kept his name clean. As much as he despised him at times, he needed Bowen.

"Well, Arnie, I hate to tell you, it's about to be an all-out war. This may be the last of our term, buddy. The governor is going to get heat brought down on him, and he's going to throw my ass from the frying pan straight into the fire." He sat back as realization set in.

Once the DETF found out that Ishmael wasn't cooperating, they'd begin to start the operations to bust and take down all major drug connects, causing an all-out war among organized drug crime and task force, all due to one knucklehead turned Al Pacino.

The rules were set in place for a reason, and anyone who did not cooperate set off a chain reaction that caused all in the game to pay. They paid by losing profit from the constant raids on their spots, which caused suppliers to tighten up on who they distributed to, which caused revenue to go down and everyone to lose big profits. Once you fuck with a man's money, you fuck with the beast in him. Ishmael would pay heavily when word got out because of his stubbornness to cooperate he would be the cause of this invasion.

The mayor would be looked upon by the public as an unfit candidate to run the city because of the turmoil that had happened, which would hinder his chances for re-election.

"I guess I'll make the call to the governor. No sense in prolonging the inevitable."

"This is bullshit, Tony. No way in fuck am I going to lose my job over some little snotty-nose punk kid. Come on. Let's think this over. There has got to be another way."

"Arnie, there is another way, but I don't want no parts of it." He looked at him sternly.

Bowen understood what he was implying.

"Shit, that's right." He pulled his chair up to the desk. "Tony, listen, I can do this. No one has to know that you had anything to do with it. Our jobs are on the line, and frankly, I can't face my wife if I lose it. I didn't bust my ass in college all those years for one nigger to pull the rug right from under my feet. I'll contact him myself this time."

"I don't know, Arnie. This could backfire, and then we would be facing prison time. No, I'll take my chances on the governor and re-election."

"Fuck! Tony, come on!" He hit the desk. He leaned forward on his hands and spoke calmly. "All I'm asking is for you to think about it. Don't make any hasty decisions yet. Go home and sleep on it, and we'll talk about this tomorrow. Okay?"

The mayor stared into the desperate eyes of his colleague and sighed. "Okay, Arnie. I'll think about."

"Good. Now let's get shit faced," Bowen said, heading toward the liquor cabinet.

CHAPTER 28

WAR

Zola and Damon lay in his bed panting like two track stars who had just completed running a fifteen-hundred-meter run. They had just finished with two hours of hot, butt-naked sexing. They had been sexing it up for the past two weeks while they planned how they were going to set up Ishmael and Derrick.

"Boo, I need some ends," Zola said.

"What?" Damon continued to pant.

"I need some money."

"Damn, you is one money-hungry bitch."

"As much as I suck you off with you busting off in my mouth, got me swallowing your babies and shit, you mean to tell me you can't kick some dollars my way?" she said, raising up off the bed.

"Yo, for real, you startin' to get on my nerves with that bitching shit." He got up off the bed, heading to the bathroom.

"Cheap-ass bastard," she said, plopping back onto the bed.

Minutes later he returned to the room.

"So what's up, Damon?"

"What?" He sounded irritated.

"When we gonna do this shit, 'cause I'm tired of begging you tired mafuckas for ya money. I want my piece of the cake."

"Stop asking me about that shit. Stick to the script and stay in yo' fucking place."

"Oh, I see what's up. You acting real grimy, nigga," she retorted.

"Man, chill out. You gon' get yo' hush money."

Zola rolled her eyes at him. She was getting real tired of him. He had been acting and talking real slick like shit was sweet like that. He didn't know who he was fucking with because on the up and up, he could get it, too, she contemplated.

Damon pulled up on the block. One of his runners approached him.

"What's good, little nigga?" he asked.

"It's all good, D! Shit poppin' like firecrackers out this mug!" he shouted.

"That's what's up." Damon nodded.

"So I heard it's 'bout to be a all-out war out this mafucka," the young boy announced.

"Fuck you talking about?"

"Yo, my sister is fucking with this cat who's down with Big Leroy, and he told her he was going to get her up outta dodge 'cause yo' boy done fucked around and stirred up some big shit downtown."

"Oh yeah?"

"Straight like that, and what's fucking wit' he said y'all niggaz 'bout to catch some serious heat. So what's up, D? We rollin' with y'all niggaz or what? 'Cause you know I'm down to pump some hot led in a mafucka," the eager boy shouted.

"Yo, man, chill. Ain't no shit like that 'bout to happen." Damon was in deep thought.

If it was about to go down, pop off like the boy said, then his work might be easier than he thought. He needed to find out what was up.

"Yo, good looking, man. That's why I fucks with you. Keep your ear to the street, and holla at a nigga when you get up on anything else," he said, giving the boy a pound and a hug.

"Word. No doubt, D. I'ma look out for you, man, 'cause you look out for me."

"A'ight. One."

Damon be-bopped back to his car and got inside. He sat in deep thought for a minute before pulling off.

Meanwhile, Ishmael, Derrick, Nate, and Dice were sitting at the garage. Nate was sucking on a blunt while Ishmael was talking.

"A'ight, I need y'all niggaz to get on your grind and dig up some real do-or-die, don't-give-a-fuck type cats. Shit about to heat up real soon. We about to get hit from all sides."

"Why we gotta do all that? We got Big Leroy on our side. That old man ain't gonna let shit go down like that," Nate said.

"Nate, put the blunt down. You ain't been listening to shit I been saying. Fuck Big Leroy. That nigga did me dirty."

"So what you saying, we on our own?" Dice inquired.

"Yeah, nigga," Derrick interjected. "Damn."

"Like I was saying, we need some real cats that fit the bill. If we gotta hold court in the streets, then so be it. Y'all niggaz gotta make it happen quick, fast, and in a hurry. You feel me?"

Everyone nodded in agreement.

"Keep this shit on the DL, and hype them clowns up on some other shit so they don't know about the real," he stated, pacing the floor.

Ishmael knew what was about to happen. He was ready for it. There was only one other dude who did the same thing he was doing, and he was a legend. It was back when he was ten years old. A dealer named Sojo Clark was one of the biggest of his time. He had running status like Frank Nitti, Nicky Barnes, and them cats had back in they time. He had shit on lock big time. Sojo didn't want to play by the rules. He had a big mouth and a lot of muscle. Sojo thought he couldn't be touched. In all actuality it was difficult to get to him. But every man is caught slipping at one time or another and can get got just like the next.

That day came when Sojo refused to cooperate with the under world, and all hell broke loose throughout the city. Enforcement came down hard on every major operation throughout the tristate area, which caused the head honchos to go after Sojo who refused to bow down.

Many innocent people lost their lives that grueling week of killings. Ishmael remembered his grandmother locking him in his bedroom to keep him from running the streets. She barricaded the apartment and kept the lights out. People ran the streets looting neighborhood stores and setting fires to cars and buildings. Gunshots rang out throughout the night. Police sirens became a way of putting people to sleep like a lullaby at night.

Hit after hit was being carried out. Ishmael couldn't sleep on the third night of that week. Every night he would pry at the burglar-proof bars that covered his bedroom window with a screwdriver until he managed to get the bottom of the gate loose. He squeezed his frail body through the bottom of the gate and dropped down one story to the grassless backyard.

He remembered running through the alleyway on the side of the house. When he stepped out onto the streets, it looked like a sight from the Vietnam War. People were running up and down the streets. Some of the local kids were setting off cherry bombs in garbage cans, sending out an ear-piercing bang.

He wandered the streets and ducked behind buildings when the police drove by. He watched a boy he went to school with get shot in the head by a stray bullet. That was the first time he ever saw a murder, and it didn't seem to bother him.

Army jeeps filled with armed guards raced through the neighborhoods. It was total chaos.

Once the smoke cleared, Sojo was a memory. It took the cities months and months to recover from the damage that was done. All the small-time hustlers came out of hiding and got right back to business, picking up the customers most of the big timers lost due to the war.

Ishmael thought about his plan carefully. If he could get some of the top doggs on his side on the strength of his rep then everything should go down smoothly. But he needed shit to pop off with a quickness.

He looked at his watch, and it was 6:30 P.M. He had to drop by the crib, shower, and change before he picked up Desiree.

"A'ight, I'm out. I'll get up with y'all later," he said, heading for the door.

"Yo, Ish, let me holla at you for a minute," Derrick yelled.

"What's up?" Ishmael asked.

"Step outside for a minute."

The two men walked out into the evening air.

"What's up?"

"You strapped?" Derrick asked.

"Yeah."

"Where you headed?"

"I'ma go see Rae. Why?"

"I don't think you should be rolling solo."

"I'm good, man." Ishmael shook Derrick's hand.

"Let me put a tail on you, man, just in case that faggot Leroy breaks new."

"I'm good, dogg. Good looking out though." Ishmael walked away.

Derrick stood there looking after his boy, not feeling him rolling without security, but that was Ishmael. He relied so much on his street credibility, confident that no one would step to him.

CHAPTER 29

IT IS ON

After Ishmael picked Desiree up, they headed over to Desiree's favorite restaurant, Oceanside, for some seafood. The two ate, drank wine, and laughed. Desiree loved his company, and Ishmael equally felt the same. They both made each other feel happy and complete. When they were together, nothing else mattered.

After dinner, Ishmael wanted to check out a movie.

"For real, Ishmael, if we go to the movies now, I know I'll fall asleep. I don't want to waste your money."

"Anything I do for you is never a waste, no matter what it is," he said as they walked hand and hand to his truck. "So what do you want to do? Anything you want to do, I'm with it."

"I want to go home and go to bed. I'm tired," she stated sincerely.

"No, I'm not ready to take you home."

"Ishmael, I need to get some rest. I'm dead on my feet right now."

He pulled her into his arms and held her tightly. "Let's go to a hotel."

"Don't get cute." She smiled up at him.

"Oh, come on. Not like that. I'm saying, we can get a nice suite. You can soak in the Jacuzzi and sip on some champagne and eat strawberries, then I can give you a nice massage. No freaky shit or nothing like that, and you can get your sleep on with no interruption. I need to get away anyway," he said.

"Hmm, sounds good, but all the Jacuzzi, champagne, and massaging definitely sounds like something freaky, and I don't care to get into that with you yet."

"Naw, Rae, I'm serious. I'm not tryna get in your drawers. What type of dude you think I am?" He looked at her mischievously.

She looked at him, and they both laughed out loud.

They arrived at the exquisite Marriott Nashua Hotel. Once they entered the room, Ishmael immediately started the water for the Jacuzzi. Desiree had to admit that she was nervous. She trusted Ishmael, but she didn't trust herself. Her imagination ran wild every time they were together, and now they were going to spend the night together.

Ishmael kept his promise and gave Desiree her space to bask in her dream getaway. Desiree nodded off several times. She decided to get out of the Jacuzzi before she really fell asleep and drowned.

She threw on one of the hotel robes that was left on the bed. When she came out of the bathroom, Ishmael laid sprawled on the king-size bed asleep. He looked so peaceful. Desiree didn't want to bother him, so she curled up next to him. Fatigue took over her body, and she drifted off to sleep.

Meanwhile Zola was sitting on the sofa at Nick D's three-bedroom ranch house an hour away from where she lived. They had been kicking it hard since the night she ran into him when she was with Nettie. She sat there sucking on a blunt when he walked in through the front door. He bounced toward her with a sly grin on his face.

Damn he is fine as hell, she thought.

The way his bow legs curved when he walked turned her on big time.

She already had plans for Nick to be the one to take Ishmael's place as soon as Damon handled his business. Nick was spoiling her already, and he was a pipe-laying fool. He satisfied her body's every craving.

He handed her the bag he received from the Chicken House restaurant. She reached inside, grabbing a chicken breast and ripping into it. Nick picked up the remote and changed the television back to MVP Baseball on PlayStation 2 before Zola got the munchies and he had to leave.

She was sitting watching him while stuffing her face when her cell phone rang. She looked at the caller ID, and it was Damon. She wasn't feeling him and didn't want Nick to know it was a dude calling her, so she pretended it was her girl Nettie.

"What's up, girl?" she asked.

"What?"

"What's up?" she repeated, looking over at Nick who was definitely engrossed in the game.

She got up off the sofa and took the bag into the kitchen.

"What Damon?" She changed her tone once she was finally in the kitchen.

"I need to get at you for a minute. I got something I need you to do. You need to meet me at the spot—now."

"No, D. I'm into something right now."

"Zo, now is not the time for this shit. If you want to do this then I need to see you. Don't have me waiting on yo' ass." He disconnected the call.

CHAPTER 30

THE DREAM

"Alright now, Rae-Rae. Don't mess this up for us," Bilal stated. It was the day of the robbery.

"What are you talking about? I know what I'm doing. Don't you fuck this up. You're the one drunk off that diesel, not me," Desiree yelled, referring to his drug use.

Bilal tried to remain calm. "Okay, Rae-Rae, I'm sorry. That's a lot of money in that other room."

"You ain't gotta tell me. So let's go get it."

It was 4:30 P.M., and security had already dropped the money off in Harry's office and left the building.

"Freeze. Put your mafucking hands where I can see them," Desiree yelled after Bilal kicked the door open.

She and Bilal were wearing ski masks as they burst into Harry's office. His assistant began to scream.

"Bitch, if you don't shut the fuck up, I'ma put one right in yo' ass," Bilal assured her.

The woman muffled her scream and began to cry. Harry sat there with his hands resting on the table with a smirk on his face.

"Well, well, lookie here. The two crackheads gonna try and rob me." He smiled, exposing their identity.

"Shut the fuck up," Desiree yelled.

Bilal began to feel uneasy as he realized their cover had been blown. The ski masks they wore didn't disguise them at all. They never considered that Harry would recognize them. But their malnutritioned bodies gave them away. Desiree moved swiftly over to the table.

"Cover me," she yelled to Bilal as she began to fill the duffle bag with money.

"How far you junkies think you're gonna get? Huh? Do you know who the fuck I am?" Harry yelled.

Desiree dropped the duffle bag and practically leaped across the table at Harry. She cracked him across the face with the gun then shoved it into his mouth.

"No, do you know who I am, you fat fuck!" She spit venom at him.

Harry began to perspire, and blood leaked from the corner of his mouth. Bilal didn't like the way this was going down. The guns were to scare Harry. He didn't intend for anyone to get hurt. Desiree was taking this too far. Desiree could tell that Bilal was ready to back out, but she wasn't having it.

"Now you shut the fuck up and nobody will get hurt," she said. Desiree swept the money from the table and into the bag.

"Let's move," she said to Bilal. "Now sit yo' fat ass still and don't move," she told Harry. "I'm gonna wait outside that door, and if I so much as hear a peep out of you, you and your bitch will catch one right between the eyes."

Desiree spotted the open safe behind the bookcase, which had been moved. She could see stacks of money lying in the safe. She tapped Bilal and pointed to the safe.

"We don't have time for that," he whispered to her.

"Fuck that," she shouted and dashed for the safe.

Desiree began raking stacks of money into the bag like a madwoman.

"Take off your jewelry," she commanded.

"Harry," his assistant whined for him to do something.

"What the fuck you calling him for? Run your jewelry, bitch," Desiree spat.

She began to help his assistant remove her jewelry.

"Get his shit," she told Bilal.

"We wasting time," he said to her.

"Just do it," she shouted.

Bilal did as he was told. Once they received the jewelry they backed slowly toward the door. Bilal flung open the door, and two security men were standing there, catching everyone by surprise. The second security team had arrived early to take the money over to the safe house. Harry had informed them earlier that day to come.

The men drew their guns, and everyone was pointing their guns at one another in a showdown stance.

One single shot was fired.

Desiree woke up in a cold sweat, screaming. She couldn't breathe from the stifling hot air that filled the room. She was soaking wet. Ishmael grabbed her and held her tight. She cried in his arms.

CHAPTER 31

CONFESSIONS

Ishmael handed her a glass of water. Desiree took a few sips and handed it back to him. He leaned his back on the headboard of the bed and pulled her into his arms.

"What time is it?" she asked.

"It's about eight o'clock in the morning. Desiree, I think it's about time you came clean with me. That was a scream from a nightmare. That sounds familiar to me."

"What do you mean, it sounds familiar?"

"I have some demons from my past that haunt me, too, and I wake up sweating and screaming just like you did. Stop fronting and tell me what's going on. The only way the nightmares are going to go away is if you face them and talk about them," he said sincerely.

"I don't want to talk about it. I'm scared, Ishmael." She began to cry.

"Baby, I know you are, but I'm here with you. Rae, I never felt this way about no woman before. There was another in my past that I thought I loved more than life itself, but since I've been with you, I don't think my love for her was as deep as what I'm feeling for you."

"You love me?" She looked at him with tears in her eyes.

"For sure." He smiled.

"Why didn't you tell me?"

"The words don't mean shit. It's the actions that say it all."

She was so impressed with him. He was so passionate and caring. She didn't admit it to him, but she had fallen in love with him a long time ago. She had to realize and come to terms with herself that Bilal was gone. Although she still loved him and thought about him, she knew Ishmael had her heart. Once he left the game then she could let go and build a relationship with him.

"So? Talk to me, Rae."

She did it. She told him about her being incarcerated for the robbery. She told him how she was sick to her stomach to have witnessed Bilal kill the security guard. She broke down and started to cry uncontrollably.

"It's gonna be a'ight, baby." He held her tightly while she cried.

He pulled her on top of him, and she straddled him and laid her head upon his chest. He rubbed her back while she whimpered.

"I ain't gonna let nothing ever happen to you, Rae. I want to one day wife you, plant my seeds, and spoil you."

She looked into his eyes. "I would love that, Ishmael, but only if you leave the streets in the streets."

He stared into her beautiful green eyes. "I'm trying, baby. I'm trying."

She leaned in and kissed his lips. He opened his mouth slightly, inviting her tongue in. They kissed deeply. He ran his hand down her back and over her ass, massaging it gently. Desiree's hormones cheered with excitement. It had been more than five years since she'd had sex. She wanted to fight the urge, but it was overwhelming.

His tool began to grow the longer they kissed. When she began to protest about his steady growing erection, he took it a step further. Ishmael rolled her over onto her back and began to kiss and suck on her neck. She moaned and held the back of his head. While kissing her neck, he loosened the belt on the robe with his other hand. He opened the robe and exposed her beautiful naked body. He ran his hand down her stomach and back up to her breasts and massaged them.

He kissed her breasts and bit her nipples lightly. Desiree moaned with pleasure. He removed her breasts and sucked and licked them seductively, circling his tongue around her rock-hard nipples.

Desiree was nervous, but she was so horny that she was ready for whatever Ishmael was working with—until he removed his Phat Farm boxers.

She couldn't believe her eyes. *Is that thing real?* she thought. Her body tightened when he began to rub her leg. All she could think of was the pain that she was about to feel. He must have felt her tense up because he began to lick her breasts again. She relaxed a little but that wasn't enough.

"I'm not going to hurt you. Just relax," he whispered in her ear.

Easy for you to say. Let me put all that up your ass, she thought.

He began to fondle her clit and finger her. Desiree forgot all about the side of beef that was waiting to enter her canal. Once she was good and wet, he climbed aboard.

It was tough going in, but he continued to kiss her neck and suck on her earlobes until he filled her canal raw dog. She flinched a couple of times, but Ishmael was a pro at finding a woman's g-spot.

They moved together, slowly meeting each other stroke for stroke, breathing together and holding each other like they never wanted to let go.

Ishmael was a talker, and he talked to her the whole time. He took his time with her, exploring her body and satisfying her over and over, orgasm after orgasm until he exploded a river of cum inside her. Neither of them said a word about not using protection. He had thought about it, but he didn't expect to have sex with her so he wasn't strapped with any condoms. Either way it was all good with him. He knew Desiree was clean, but she couldn't say the same for him.

Ishmael collapsed on top of her after their second time making love. He was a thoroughbred that day. He never was able to go that long with Zola unless he had been smoking weed and drinking.

He lay on his back, and Desiree curled up in his arms. He realized why he'd never lasted as along with Zola. It was because he fucked Zola, but he made love to Desiree, and that was the difference.

His cell phone had rang several times when they first got to the hotel but he let it ring and then finally turned it off. He wanted to spend quality time with Desiree, and that he did.

CHAPTER 32

THE HIT MAN

The mayor drove his classic mint-green convertible Mercedes SLK32 with the butterscotch soft leather interior into the parking garage. He pulled into the space marked RESERVED—MAYOR ONLY. He sat behind the wheel staring at the cement wall. He didn't get a wink of sleep the night before, thinking about all the fiascos that could possibly happen. He tossed and turned until his wife asked him to go sleep on the couch. She had an early morning court appearance scheduled, and he was causing her to lose sleep.

Just two stories up in a conference room located in the rear of the building, Arnold Bowen and a man were sitting at a table.

"So do you understand what predicament this puts the mayor in?" Bowen asked.

"Yes, I do," the unidentified Hispanic man said.

He was a hit man Bowen had used in the past.

"Will it be a problem for you to take care of this issue?"

"If the price is right, no, it wouldn't be a problem," the Hispanic man said.

"Good." Bowen stood to his feet. "Is the price still the same?"

"No." The gentleman laughed. "No way, not for this one."

Bowen looked at the man with strange eyes. "What the hell is so special about this punk? Why does everyone seem to walk on their toes when it comes to this ass wipe? What the hell kind of a kid is he?" Bowen shouted.

The visitor continued to laugh. "He's your worst nightmare in disguise. He's like a thief in the night. You will never see him coming until it's too late. Besides, I owe him one."

"You owe him one? Do you know this punk?"

"Let's just say we loved the same woman," the hit man stated.

"So your revenge is over a woman?" Bowen asked, confused.

"Not just any woman. She was my sister." The man stared off into space.

"Was your sister?"

"Yeah, he killed her. Her name was Sasha."

The elevator doors opened, and the mayor stepped off. He seemed to be staring off into space as he walked through the corridors of City Hall.

"Good morning, Mr. Mayor," a woman said.

He gave her a slight smile and gracious nod.

"Morning, Mr. Mayor," a gentleman said, passing by.

"George," he responded.

He walked by his secretary, not acknowledging her. He sat behind his huge desk. He grabbed the pen that sat there and began to tap it on the desk like a drum before snatching up his phone and dialing a number.

"Hello."

"Leroy, are you in your office?"

"Yes."

"I'll be there in twenty minutes."

"You're slumming today?"

"Just be there when I get there." He disconnected the call.

Twenty minutes later the mayor was sitting in Leroy's office in the rear of the pool hall.

"Leroy, I've known you for many years," he said, loosening his tie. "I was the snot-nose kid you use to hand twenty-dollar bills to when you came into my father's car dealership. I used to think you were the cleanest cat I'd ever seen. I can't thank you enough for what you've done for me in the past. Now that I'm in office, you and I have been doing business for quite some time. You've scratched my back, and I've scratched yours."

"Where you going with all this, Tony?" Leroy interrupted.

"Come on, Leroy. My nuts are in a grinder right now. The governor is riding me like a bull at a rodeo. Talk to the kid. Let him know what can happen," he pleaded.

"Tony," Leroy sang, "he knows what can happen, and frankly, I think he'll come out on top when this all blows over."

"What? Are you insinuating that you urged him to do this?"

"No. I didn't ass-inuate anything. Let me tell you something." Leroy leaned forward on his elbows. "This kid as you call him is very much a man—a very, very dangerous man. Hell, I took a chance at what I did to him."

"What do you mean what you did to him?"

"That don't matter right now, but what does matter is the street credibility this young man has. He's got a lot of respect, and respect will back him any day."

"Listen to me, Leroy." The mayor took off his tie and jacket. He unbuttoned the top button of his shirt. "No more shitting around with you. Let me talk your language." He was getting pissed. The lines in his forehead deepened. His face became flush.

"Bring it. I knew you still had some nigger in you. I ain't believe you was a tight ass all the time," Leroy said, laughing.

The mayor ignored his arrogance. "You were here when Sojo tried to pull that same bullshit. You saw what happened? Now I happen to know a whole hell of a lot more than you think I know."

"Oh yeah." Leroy chuckled, unconvinced that the mayor had anything on him. If anything, Leroy thought, he had a whole pile of shit on *him*.

"Yeah." He smirked. "I know that kid is your son. He wasn't Willie Jenkins' boy; he's yours."

Willie Jenkins was known to all to be Ishmael's father.

The mayor sat back and watched Leroy's smile turn into dumbfoundedness. "Did I hit a spot, homeboy? You were fucking that boy's mother while she tricked for Willie. When she found out she was pregnant, you told her to tell Willie it was his baby because you knew what Willie would have done to your backstabbing ass if he found out. You were supposed to have been his boy and you were fucking his bottom whore. You were always jealous of him. He had more status than you did. Even though he pimped and you was a pusher he still outshined you any day."

"That's bullshit," Leroy said, not believing it was.

"Yeah, it's bullshit alright. You two figured since you and Willie resembled that it wouldn't make any difference what the boy looked like because Willie would believe it was his."

"Where did you get that bullshit from?"

"That don't matter, but what matters is that boy is your own flesh and blood. How could you be so coldhearted? You mean to tell me you would let him pay for his own suicide ticket? Leroy, you always been a greedy fuck. What would you get out of the deal if this kid dies?"

Leroy didn't say a word he stared at the mayor like he was crazy.

"I know you care about him. I know how you nurtured him and took care of him. I also know you had something to do with Willie's murder because he turned that boy's mother into a junkie. You tried like hell to clean her up, but when she OD'd, you lost it. I can't prove it, but there's a lot of information about it. You had Willie murdered." He pointed at him.

Leroy lit a cigar and began to perspire. The mayor knew a little too much about his secrets. He wondered what else he knew. Leroy knew one thing, he needed to maintain his cool.

"I don't want to put any idle threats on you, Leroy."

"Then don't," Leroy said.

"But—" he put his hand up to stop him—"hear me out. I just want you to know what I'm working with. That's your son, Leroy. Don't let him do this. Talk to him again. That's all I'm asking," he said, standing to his feet.

The mayor picked up his tie and suit jacket and threw them over his arm.

"Just talk to him, Leroy. Let him know this is the better way."

With that said and done, the mayor walked out of the office.

Leroy wiped his forehead with the palm of his hand. He leaned back in his chair and stared at the ceiling. The mayor was telling the truth. Ishmael was his son. Leroy was in love with Ishmael's mother, Regina. He had had a crush on her for years. He and Willie were tight growing up. Willie wasn't much of a hustler. He was always a ladies' man. He was a black knight in shining armor to any woman. He was smooth and sexy. He had good looks, and he knew that he could talk a woman out of her panties any day. Willie was a well-known pimp with a lot of street credibility.

Willie knew Leroy always liked Regina. Leroy was pissed when he found out Willie had abducted her into his stable of whores. Regina was a dime piece. Every man wanted to wife her, but Willie saw her potential to make his pockets fat, so he stepped to her before Leroy had the chance.

For a long time, Leroy tried to get with her, but Willie had a tight hold on her. Willie had a lot of pull in the city, and Leroy knew it. He was jealous and envious of Willie. Leroy felt he was the baller getting major paper so he should've had more pull than Willie, but he didn't. Instead of fighting against his long-time friend, he chose to creep around with his bottom bitch.

When Regina came up pregnant, they both knew it was his baby. She didn't sleep with any man—including Willie—without protection.

Leroy remembered a time when Willie had this cat beaten to a bloody pulp because he tried to have a relationship with Regina. The dude took her away for the weekend one time, showering her with gifts, trying to turn a whore into a housewife. Once Willie found out where they were, he sent his squad out after them. Leroy was there the day they brought them back to the house. The man was near death, and Leroy almost lost his lunch looking at the condition the man was in. He definitely didn't want that to happen to him if Willie found out that Regina was carrying his baby.

Regina couldn't get an abortion because that would mean she would have to deal with Willie and all the questions he would ask about her pregnancy, so she devised a plan to sabotage the condom the next time they had sex. When they finally had sex, the condom broke. Several weeks later she informed him of her pregnancy, and the rest is history.

CHAPTER 33

POPPED CHERRY

Desiree walked into the house that afternoon only to meet Beverly sitting at the kitchen table.

"Un-huh, bitch. I see you got your cherry popped today."

"What are you talking about, Bev?" She smiled.

"I'm talking about that big-ass grin you got on your face telling all your business," she said, laughing.

"You don't know what you're talking about. I gotta get me some sleep before I go to work," Desiree said, walking out of the kitchen.

Beverly hopped up and followed right on her heels. "So how was it?"

"How was what, Bev?"

"Oh, don't play stupid. Is Ish holding or what?" she blurted out.

"Beverly!" Desiree was shock at what she just said. "Okay, you are a trip."

"What? Ain't no shame in my game. You should know that by now. Stop tryna change the subject because I know you was with Ish all night. And ain't no female gonna spend the night with a nigga and not get her salad tossed." Beverly stood with her hands on her hips.

"Oh my God, Beverly." Desiree put her hand over her mouth. "How the hell do you know who I was with?"

"You forgot? I'm the four-one-one of the hood."

Both women burst into laughter as they plopped down on the bed. Desiree told Beverly everything—that she had the best sex she had ever had in her entire life.

"See, I told you he was a good man. He ain't like them other busters out there, Rae-Rae. Look at you, glowing and shit."

Desiree smiled from ear to ear.

"So when are you gonna run his pockets and get some of that cheddar?" Beverly inquired.

"Okay, see now you know you wrong for that. That's not why I like him, Bev." She rolled her eyes.

The horn of Beverly's boyfriend's truck blew, interrupting their sister-girl conversation. Beverly dashed to the window.

"I'm coming," she yelled out.

"Okay, Rae-Rae, I'll see you later, and trust we will finish this conversation." She pointed at her in a motherly way.

"Bye, Beverly." Desiree waved. "Oh, Bev!"

"What now?" Beverly turned around.

"Leave the door unlocked. Ishmael is coming over."

"You ain't get enough last night?" Beverly smiled and walked out.

Desiree lay across her bed and gazed up at the ceiling with a smile on her face. She was indeed happy. She loved Ishmael, and he told her he loved her. He was right. You can show a person your love without using words. She began to relax and sleep took over.

CHAPTER 34

THE SHOWDOWN

"Drop your weapons," security yelled.

"No, you drop your fucking weapons," Bilal yelled back.

Desiree began to get nervous. She knew then that they were not going to come out of the situation alive. If she would have just stuck to the plan, they would have been long gone. She had messed up, and she knew it.

Harry's laughter roared from the office.

"Oh yeah! Now what you gonna do?" he shouted.

Desiree's hand began to shake, losing the firm grip she once had. Her mind began to race thinking of a way out of the situation.

Both the security guards were cock diesel and clearly weren't backing down. Someone had to make a move first.

It seemed like it all happened in slow motion. Bilal capped off into the head of the security guard who stood in front of him. The large man fell to the floor hard. The other guard looked down at his dead friend when Desiree snapped out of her stupor and kicked the big man square in the nuts.

He growled a body-shivering yell and grabbed his crotch. Bilal grabbed Desiree by the arm, and they bolted for the steps. They could hear Harry's assistant and Harry screaming as they ran.

They ran through the bowling alley as onlookers watched. Making it out the rear entrance, they escaped through the alley and onto the side street.

They removed their masks and ran for their lives. A cab drove past them, and Bilal flagged it to stop. They jumped in, ducking down.

Breathing heavily, they both slowly looked out the rear window of the cab, seeing if anyone was coming. No one was in sight, and they both lay back onto the seat. Desiree's mouth began to water. She rolled down the window and leaned out to throw up.

Bilal instructed the cabbie to take them to a local motel. They checked in and headed for their room. Once inside Desiree raced to the bathroom and threw up again. Her stomach was nervous. She had never done anything like that in her life. She would have never thought of robbing anyone in all the years of her life, let alone actually committing the crime. The day Roc and Tracey were killed in their apartment reappeared in her mind.

When she came out of the bathroom, Bilal had dumped the contents of the bag onto the bed. There was a huge pile of bundled money and the jewelry they lifted. She looked at the contents and smiled.

"We did it, babe," Bilal whispered.

"We sure did," she said just as quietly.

They began to count the money. When they finished the total came to $210,000. That was more money than either of them had seen at one time.

"Rae-Rae, I'm gonna go cop us a little celebration," Bilal stated, getting up from the bed.

"No, Bunchy. Don't go."

"Rae-Rae, it's alright, babe. They don't know where we're at, and by the time they get a whiff of where we're at, we'll be long gone. We'll stay here the night and get on the next thing smoking in the morning. Okay?" he said, reassuring her.

"I don't know, Bunchy. I'm scared."

"I know, babe, but don't worry. We a long way from Fifteenth Avenue, and that's the first place they'll look. I'll be right back. I know a spot four or five blocks from here."

Desiree didn't say a word. She just looked at him with frightful eyes. He walked over to her, pulling her to her feet. He embraced her tightly. She began to cry. Bilal stroked her head and rocked her back and forth. He broke their embraced, reached onto the bed, grabbed a stack of money, and walked out of the hotel room. There was only one thing on his mind, and he was determined to get it.

Desiree tried to watch TV to take her mind off the day's events. It was still early and dusk outside. She would have much rather Bilal waited until after dark before he went out.

There was nothing interesting on TV so she put the money back into the bag, zipping it up. She threw the bag onto a chair that sat in the room. She lay across the bed, trying to think of anything other than the images of Roc, Tracey, and the bullet hole in the security guard's head that kept reappearing in her mind.

Fifteen minutes had gone by, but it seemed like an eternity to Desiree. Every time she heard a noise or a voice, she would run to the window and peek out of the curtain. Her stomach began to quiver—she'd had the runs since Bilal left. The anticipation of a hit was getting the best of her. She pulled the chair in front of the window and peeked out of it. After a few minutes, she spotted Bilal walking briskly toward the motel. She jumped up and went to the door, opening it. He hurried in with two huge bags and a large bag of White Castle hamburgers. The other bags were filled with junk food, sodas, beers, and the paraphernalia they needed to get high.

For the next three days, Bilal and Desiree stayed in the motel room and got high. Although that wasn't the initial plan, since they were addicts, once they started getting high they couldn't stop, and time flew by. During those days at the motel Desiree even coerced Bilal into smoking coke.

Finally on the morning of the fourth day, reality set in. They lay awake watching the news, taking a break from getting high, when the report on the robbery at Groovers I appeared on the screen. A sketch of Bilal and Desiree was plastered across the television. They both were wanted for armed robbery and murder. The sketches were very accurate, and fear settled into Bilal's heart.

"Rae-Rae! We gotta go now!"

Desiree didn't move. She was in shock.

Bilal continued to watch the news while he put on his clothes. The news report had an accurate description on what he and Desiree were last seen wearing as well. Bilal hit himself upside the head. If he had been thinking, he would have purchased them some different clothing while he was out. He could've kicked his own ass for not sticking to the plans of only staying one night at the motel. He sat down on the side of the bed to think about their next move.

Desiree still sat in shock as she stared at the picture of herself on the TV screen. "What are we gonna do, Bunchy?"

"I don't know, Rae-Rae. Let me think a minute."

"We could stay here, Bunchy. They don't know where we are. We could stay in the room, and nobody would know. We got enough money to pay for the room for a year," she reasoned, not thinking clearly.

"And what are we supposed to do when we want to get high, Rae-Rae?"

She didn't think about that. She could go a couple of days without cocaine, but Bilal would keel over and die if he didn't get his fix. He would surely be sick.

"Plus, Rae-Rae, we ain't let them clean this room in three days. They gonna start getting suspicious soon. No, Rae-Rae, we gotta leave. We'll walk down to that thrift store a few blocks away and get some new clothes. We need a disguise," he said, rushing around and putting things away.

Desiree got out of the bed and began to dress as well. Once they were dressed and everything was packed away, they headed out of the door. On the second night at the hotel Bilal had gone to the office and paid for the additional night. Bilal left the key on the dresser in the room. He didn't feel the need to return it. He wanted as little face-to-face contact as possible.

As they entered into the thrift shop, an elderly black woman with white hair appeared from the back room.

"Good day. May I help you?" she asked.

Desiree was nervous, and it clearly showed. Bilal held her hand and squeezed it for reassurance. With a smile on his face, he told the woman they were just looking and he'd let her know when they were ready.

They found and purchased new clothing as well as hats and shoes to go with the outfits. The elderly woman even allowed them to use her back room to change, and Bilal rewarded her with a hefty tip. They thanked the woman and left. Desiree felt much better once they were disguised.

They caught a cab and made a beeline straight for Penn Station to catch a train out of state. After they purchased their tickets, they sat in the back of the station, staying clear of the center of attention. It would be one hour and forty-five minutes until boarding time. It couldn't come soon enough for Desiree. She kept having an eerie felling in the pit of her stomach. She would feel much better once they were on the train and moving.

One hour later, they prepared themselves to go to the track where the Amtrak train would be boarding. Once they arrived, they walked down the platform, away from the other passengers. Bilal tried to strike up a conversation to keep her mind off things.

Fifteen minutes had gone by when Desiree spotted two distinguished white men in business suits walking onto the platform. They were clean cut and neat. They appeared to be looking for someone. She grabbed Bilal's arm and pulled him back up against the wall.

"What's wrong, Rae-Rae?"

"Look down there. Do those two white men look like cops to you?" She pointed.

Bilal leaned forward to look then leaned back. "You being paranoid. Calm down. They're probably just businessmen. They ride the train too."

"Bunchy, it's ninety-five degrees outside, and they got on three-piece suits with tight-ass ties choking their necks."

"Yeah, you're right."

Bilal pulled his brim down farther on his head as Desiree did the same with her hat. They clutched each other and pressed their bodies up against the wall.

Little did they know, the detectives had been hot on their trail since the start. They arrived shortly after Bunchy and Desiree left the scene of crime that day at Groovers. Just that morning the cabbie came forward with information after seeing the news. He told them that he dropped them off at the motel. The detectives went to the motel and showed the desk clerk the sketches. He identified them and took the detectives to the room where they found it empty. The detectives went up and down to the different businesses north and south on that street inquiring if anyone had seen them.

Harry told the detectives that Desiree and Bilal were addicts and that they would have to come out sooner or later to cop. The detectives had gone around to all the drug spots within a five-mile radius of the bowling alley, asking about the two. Of course, no one said anything.

Finally, they came up on a lead when they stopped by the thrift store to ask questions. The old lady cooperated with the detectives. She told them that Desiree and Bilal were there earlier and she heard the two talking while they were in back changing clothes. She said she heard them say something about going to Virginia.

They radioed in to have police posted at the airport while they went to the train station. They had police question passengers, showing the sketches of Desiree and Bilal. The police officers searched the bathrooms, while the two detectives searched each platform for scheduled trains heading for Pennsylvania.

The two men had searched one side of the platform and were heading in their direction. They walked up on them and asked if they'd seen the people in the two pictures. Neither Bilal nor Desiree would lift their heads high enough to show their full faces.

"No," they both replied together.

The two detectives began to walk away, satisfied with their answer when one of the detectives spotted the duffel bag that sat on the platform that read Groovers I on the side.

"Alright, put your hands in the air and turn around and face the wall!"

Desiree woke up in a cold sweat. Ishmael was sitting in the chair next to her bed. He sat on the bed and pulled her into his arms. Neither said a word. She couldn't take the nightmares anymore. She wished she could be with Ishmael. Desiree thought about telling him about when Roc and Tracey were murdered. Although she told him about the robbery, she didn't tell him about that. Ishmael did say she had to talk about it in order to move on. But she was afraid so she just lay there in his arms.

CHAPTER 35

TEAM UP

Ishmael and Derrick walked into Imani's, a soul food restaurant. The doorman recognized the men and escorted them up the stairs to the second level. They walked down the narrow hallway to the rear door. Ishmael opened the door, and he and Derrick walked into a room filled with smoke. All the leaders of each territory they claimed along with their protégés were there. Ishmael had called this meeting to talk to them about the goings-on downtown. He wanted opinions and assistance, if needed, to support what he was about to do.

He shook hands with everyone. Ishmael didn't nor did he ever have any beef with any of the leaders. People of Ishmael's status and men who ranked equal to Leroy were in attendance. They ranged from North to South Jersey to Philly.

There were also some rival members present, but the rules were whenever a meeting was called, all beefs were set aside. Business was business, and that was that.

Ishmael didn't waste any time. He got right down to the business at hand.

"Gentleman, I know some of you may have already heard some shit about me. I called this meeting to be straight up with you and tell you what's going down with me. No rumor can put it out there on the real, so

I called you all here to clear my name and to discuss some things I want to do."

Everyone gave Ishmael his undivided attention. Ishmael looked around the room into each of their faces before he continued, to make sure he had their attention.

The top men in attendance were Walter "Watts" Oaks of Atlantic City, running Atlantic county; David "The Don" Lewis of Paterson, running Bergen county; Eric "E" Evans of Camden, running Camden county; Craig "C-Mack" Fulton of New Brunswick, running Middlesex county; Gary "The Villain" Smith of Philly, running Philadelphia county; Isaac "Hype" Dixson of Jersey City, running Hudson County; and Johnny "Jo-Jo" Donalds of Elizabeth, running Union County. Missing from the meeting was Leroy "Big Roy" Wilson, running Essex County.

"I know you heard that I refused to give up a cut of my profits."

Some of the members looked at one another in shock and some began to whisper to one another.

"Now hold up. Before you go getting shit twisted. I have my reasons. How long have those mafuckas downtown in your area been making a profit off your operations?" Not waiting for an answer, he continued. "For years, right? I know it goes far back as at least when I was a kid."

They nodded in agreement.

"Well, when does the shit stop? I mean we still slaving for these mafuckas, and the last time I checked, slavery is over."

"Young fella, I hear what you're saying, but ain't nothing wrong with giving up a little to get a lot," E from Camden stated.

"No disrespect, E, but you getting ten percent from the people under you to protect them and you giving the other thirty-five percent to mafuckas downtown in your city to give to the fucking governor. While your people take a loss, you still gain. What type of shit is that?" Ishmael inquired.

The protégés all looked at one another and agreed.

"I ain't saying not to give them anything. I mean yeah, we need to keep them off our ass, but what I'm saying is we need to change the rules a little bit. We need to lower the pay, and if they don't roll with that, then fuck 'em. We just hold court in the streets."

"Naw, young gunner, I ain't with going through all that bullshit all over again. I went through that shit when I lived here with that crazy-ass Sojo. You need to re-evaluate the situation and ante up. Besides, this here beef is on y'all. I ain't even livin' in Jersey," Villain from Philly growled.

Ishmael leaned back in his chair. This was going to be harder than he thought. They all sat around and went back and forth about what was the right way and what was the wrong way, who was too old and too tired to fight and who would go in with him. Ishmael knew he wouldn't be able to convince all of them, but if he could at least get half of them on his side, he would be set.

"A'ight, so right now Watts and The Don are down with me. Is there anybody else?"

No one gave a signal. Ishmael stood.

"I have never had a problem with any of you. My credibility on the streets is straight. My father ran with some of you. You mean to tell me y'all would rather bow down than to stand up straight like men?"

"Ishmael," C-Mack said, standing, "this ain't got nothing to do with bowing down. I'm gettin' money, and I ain't about to fuck that up on some ole bullshit. I wish you luck, kid." He walked toward the door with his protégé on his heels.

One by one they began to stand. The Villain, Jo-Jo, and E all walked out wishing him luck as they exited. Hype remained seated along with Watts and the Don. Hype and Watts were two of the youngest tops doggs. Both their fathers were in leadership positions before they were killed, therefore passing the rank down to them. They were wild gun-busting-type niggas. The Don was an OG who hated the police so he would be down for anything.

"Let me ask you something, Ish," Hype said.

"Kick it."

"What's the problem with paying the percentage?"

"The problem is, we taking all the risks and them cracker mafuckas is buying they wives chinchillas and taking them on fucking cruises and shit."

"Can't you afford to buy your lady a chinchilla and take her on a cruise?" Hype asked.

"Yeah, so what's your point?" Ishmael inquired.

"That's my point. You still getting paper, and you acting greedy. A greedy hand is a dead hand," Hype schooled.

"Hype, it ain't about the money. It's the GP."

"I hope you're ready for what you about to start, homey."

"So are you with me or not?"

"I'm with you, 'cause I like your style. I've always admired the way you made Leroy a rich nigger. By the way, where is he?"

Although Ishmael wanted to diss the hell out of Leroy, he didn't. He lived by the code of the streets, so he lied so as not to dog Leroy's name. A man's rep is all he has.

"He had business to take care of." Ishmael looked away.

CHAPTER 36

SNAKIN

Zola walked into the house she and Ishmael shared. She had just come from spending the rest of her night with Damon. She hated that she had to keep leaving Nick D and go meet up with Damon for stupid shit that didn't have anything to do with making Ishmael disappear.

Damon put her down on what was going on with Ishmael. He schooled her on what she needed to do to complete her part in it. Of course he used that excuse to get her to come over to his crib so he could hit it, when he could've told her the information over the phone. She was real tired of him and no longer wanted to deal with him, but she needed him.

She walked into the bedroom. She hadn't been staying at the house much. She'd been hanging tough with Nick. Ishmael was never home anyway. She had to admit to herself that she did miss him a little.

She lay across the bed and kicked off her stilettos. Her cell phone began to ring.

"What's up?"

"What's up, Zo?" her friend Nettie asked. "Where you at?"

"I'm at the crib. Why, what's up?"

"I'm on my way," Nettie announced.

"What's up?" Zola repeated.

"I'll tell when I get there. Oh, where Ish at? He there?"

"No. I don't know where he is. I'm waiting for him to call me back. I called his cell and left him a message," she responded.

"A'ight. I'm on my way." The line went dead.

Zola went downstairs and sat in the living room to wait for Nettie.

"So what's up? Why the urgency?" Zola asked Nettie as she walked in.

"Your man is snaking." Nettie pointed at her.

"What?"

"Yeah. I heard he was fucking with some square bitch with long hair and green eyes."

Zola looked at her girl, confused. Ishmael had always been loyal to her. He had never stepped outside of their relationship. She knew he wasn't the type to cluck around with the chicken heads who flew around in the coop. Although she wasn't in love with him, she did care a little for him.

Hearing what Nettie just told her did something to her. Although she cheated on Ishmael on the regular, she felt he had no right to do her dirty. She had accused him of cheating several times before but she really never believed it. She knew she had him in the palm of her hand. The nerve of him to try and play her.

"How you know that?" she asked.

"Mafuckas talk, Zo. Shit, up in the strip joint you hear everything." She kicked off her shoes and put her feet up onto the sofa. "At first when I heard this chick named Rita say she saw him with the green-eyed bitch, I didn't think anything of it, but then she kept talking about it, 'cause you know a lot of bitches is on his dick."

Zola continued to stare at her, not believing her ears.

"I don't see what y'all bitches see in his ugly ass. Anyway, she kept going on and on about how when she found out y'all broke up that she was tryna push up on him but he wasn't biting."

"Broke up? Who said we broke up?" Zola was shocked.

"I don't know. I guess that's the word on the street. Let me finish telling you."

"Go 'head then," Zola yelled, clearly hurt.

"She said she saw him a couple of times with the new chick and that pissed her off. And check this out—" she patted Zola on her knee—"Rita works at the Marriott on day shift in housekeeping—you know, cleaning rooms. So she said she was going into the laundry room with some sheets."

Zola waved her hand to edge her to hurry up and get to the point.

"A'ight, damn. Just chill out and listen." Zola rolled her eyes. "So she said she see all kinds of people coming through the lobby checking in and out. Well low and behold coming up off the elevator was Ishmael with that bitch. She said she almost shitted in her pants when she saw him, so she went and checked the register and that dumb ass signed his real name. And yes, Zo, they was there all night."

"How you know she's telling the truth?"

Nettie cocked her head sideways. "Now I know you ain't gonna sit there and act like you sweet on that nigga."

"Hell no. Don't get it twisted. I'm saying he tryna play me."

"That's what I'm talking about. Now I know you ain't gonna let that go down," Nettie instigated. "What you gonna do? Because whatever it is, I want in."

"I don't know, Nettie, damn. Do you think Rita can find out where this tramp rest at?"

"I don't know if she can, but I know who can."

"Who?"

"The four-one-one of the hood—Bev."

"Oh, that's right. If don't nobody else know, Beverly will definitely know," Zola agreed.

"Good. That's what's up. Now let's get that mafucka," Nettie announced.

"Naw, not yet, Nett."

"What? Let me find out that you sprung." Nettie looked at her in disbelief.

Zola was vexed. She wanted revenge, and revenge she was going to get, but she didn't want to mess up what Damon had in store for Ishmael. But she was definitely going to find out if all Nettie had just told her was true.

"So you just gonna let that bum-ass nigga slide, huh?" Nettie waited for a response.

"No, but check it, I got something else planned for his ass."

She decided to tell Nettie what was about to go down and how Damon was in the mix. Nettie was all for it. She couldn't stand Ishmael. She didn't care too much for Damon either, but if it was to get rid of Ishmael, she was with it. Not to mention Zola said she was gonna break her off a little something for being a down bitch and having her back.

CHAPTER 37

DOWNTOWN

Bowen walked into the room where they played cards every week-end. As usual Cohen was flipping off at the mouth.

"Arnie boy, what's up?" He imitated a homeboy, bopping his head, using hand motions. "What's going down, my man?"

He looked totally awkward, and Bowen didn't see the humor, whereas the rest burst into laughter. The men had already started drinking before he got there, and it was obvious they were feeling good.

"Where you been, Arnie? I haven't seen you in a while," Littleton inquired.

"I've been busy with the mayor's campaign, getting ready for the election." Bowen sat down in his usual spot across from Cohen.

"We missed you for the last couple of weeks. You know Cohen blew our asses out of the water. My wife is threatening to kick me out of the house because this cock sucker keeps sending me home broke." Littleton laughed.

"Yeah, Arnie, I missed taking your money too. Ante up, fellas," Cohen yelled.

The men drank and played several hands. As usual when Cohen was over his drinking limit, he started in on Bowen.

"Did Tony talk to the old man, Arnie boy?" he slurred.

Bowen cleared his throat. "Our young friend will be a memory soon enough."

"Memory?" Weston inquired.

"Yeah, memory," Bowen stated, looking directly into the hand he held. The men looked at one another with confusion.

"What the hell are you talking about?" Cohen belted out loudly. "Did the son of a bitch die or something?"

"He said he will be a memory *soon,* Cohen," Weston repeated, "so that means he's still alive."

"Is he planning on dying soon or something?" Littleton asked. "Oh, don't tell me you got some illegal crap going on, Arnie. I don't want nothing to do with that."

Bowen looked at him like he was crazy. "All this shit is illegal, Tom. I'm not doing anything illegal."

"So what the fuck are you talking about?" Cohen yelled.

"Forget it. The kid has agreed to pay," Bowen lied.

Cohen looked at him with unbelieving eyes. He may have been wasted, but he was smart.

"Hey, fellas, don't pay him no attention. He's shit faced." Cohen laughed, still looking at Bowen. "Right, bro?" He laughed again.

Littleton and Weston joined in on the joke. Bowen was not laughing.

The men staggered to their cars in the underground garage. They were loud and drunk.

"See you guys on Monday," Cohen yelled out. "Hey, Arnie, wait up." He staggered as he walked.

"You sure you're alright to drive?" Bowen asked.

"Shit yeah. That car of mine knows its way home without my help."

He threw his huge arm around Bowen's narrow shoulder, causing him bend from the weight.

"You sneaky son of a bitch." Cohen pointed his finger in Bowen's face. His breath was hot and reeked of bourbon. "I know what you're up to," he sang.

"You're drunk, Bobby. Go home and sleep it off." Bowen held him up.

"Not as drunk as you think I am. I want in. I know what you're about to do. Don't forget I was a part of the last project you did. Remember?" he slurred.

How could Bowen forget? Cohen took more than half the profit. Four years ago they had a small-time dealer who was on the rise. He became cocky and didn't want to cooperate. The young man was sloppy and careless, but he profited a lot of revenue. He was becoming a serious problem, and the murder rate shot up in the city. The police couldn't bust him doing anything, and it brought a lot of heat on the mayor. Bowen then took matters into his own hands like he always did to protect the mayor and hired a hit man to do the job, and he figured he would take whatever drug money they found to keep for himself.

But what Bowen didn't expect was Cohen to show up. Cohen had been tailing the young dealer for a month, and he was casing the man's residence when Bowen and his hit man showed up.

The hit man was like a snake, quiet and smooth. Cohen had never seen anything like it. He slithered in the bushes until the dealer came home. Once the dealer exited the car, the hit man floated up to him, not making a sound. He slit the young man's throat so quick and quiet that the man didn't have time to scream.

He watched Bowen exit the van and help the hit man take the body inside. Cohen got out of his vehicle and walked into the opened door, walking in on Bowen's adventure.

"Bobby, there is no project. Go home, buddy. Sleep it off, okay?" Bowen smiled at him.

"Yeah, okay, Arnie boy." He patted Bowen's face.

Cohen staggered off toward his car. He fell down and rolled onto his back and started laughing. Bowen was going to go over and help him but decided not to.

He hopped into his car and sped away, leaving Cohen lying on the garage floor.

CHAPTER 38

CREEPIN

Ishmael was sitting at the stash house, waiting for his security men and the deliveryman to come by. He never touched any of the product. Ishmael only dealt with the money. He'd used the same four men for years. The only time he saw the deliveryman was when it was time to pick up and deliver. He paid him and his security team well, and they respected him to the utmost. They would do anything for Ishmael.

Ishmael had made contact and had a sit-down with the new connect who was bringing the new heroin over from Cuba. The details were discussed, and the deal was sealed. After he and Leroy bumped heads that day in his office, Ishmael no longer wanted to deal with Leroy's suppliers. He had intentions on putting Leroy down on the new product, but that changed when Leroy kicked his back in.

Nate and Dice was posted up in the corner of the room rolling dice. Derrick was on his cell phone talking to some chick Ishmael hadn't met. Although he'd never seen her before, he figured she had to be cool if Derrick was dealing with her. Ishmael looked at his watch. It was 12:30 A.M. He pulled his cell phone out and called Desiree at work. They talked for a few minutes until his other line beeped. He told her he'd call her back and clicked over. It was his deliveryman.

Five minutes later, the four men walked into the house. Nate went into the back room and came out with a garbage bag, which contained the buy money. It was then counted again so that everyone knew how much was there. Rubber bands were then wrapped around the money, and it was placed into a duffel bag.

Once the product was picked up, it was then taken to the drop house where his lieutenants met up and began to bag up the product. A portion of the bagged product was then delivered to the other states Ishmael had on lock. Ishmael's entire operation brought in more than three hundred g's a week. But with the new product, he was sure to gross over five hundred grand a week.

Everyone went their separate ways. Derrick was parked out front of a strip club called Bodacious. He watched as the girls filed out, all heading home for the night. Nettie walked out of the club and spotted him sitting in his truck across the street. She smiled and pranced over to the truck, walking up to the driver side window.

"What are you doing here?" She smiled, showing her deep dimples.

"I came to see if you wanted to get into something, maybe go get some chow," Derrick said, staring deep into her eyes.

"Well, I was about to go home. I'm tired. You want to come with me?" She flirted.

He just stared at her with a slight smirk. That was good for him because he hardly ever smiled.

Derrick had wanted to get with Nettie since the first time he met her with Zola, but he knew his boy couldn't stand her, so he chilled. Ishmael didn't listen to him when he gave his opinion about Zola, and he never knew why. Ishmael said Nettie wasn't shit. He trusted his boy's judgment.

Derrick had run into her the other day, which was very strange because he rarely saw Nettie out in the streets. It wasn't like they hung out at the same places, and Derrick was pretty much a low-key guy. Every now and then he might get with some old jump-offs to release a pound of cum, but nonetheless they didn't cross paths.

When he ran into her, they sat and talked for a long time. She was clearly pushing up on him, and he was feeling her vibes. She admitted she knew how Ishmael felt about her, which was why she was never around anymore when Zola was with them. She also admitted she felt the same way about him, but on the strength of her girl, she chilled.

Derrick didn't like that she was a dancer, but Nettie told him she needed the extra money to go back to school, which she had no intention of doing.

"So what's up? You gonna swing by or not?"

"Go get in your car. I'll follow you," he stated calmly.

She walked off back across the street to her car, throwing her ass from side to side. Nettie knew she had it going on. Her ass was perfectly shaped, and she had the best set of legs a woman can have. Derrick leaned forward to get a better look at her onion until she got into the car.

CHAPTER 39

SUCKING UP

Ishmael was on his way to chill with Derrick since they hadn't hung out lately. Ishmael wanted to rap with him about his new flame, but before going, he swung by Beverly's crib to talk to Desiree for a while. She asked him for some loot to put down on an apartment she had been looking at in Elizabeth. It felt good to him that she finally put her pride aside and asked for his help.

He admired her being independent and all, but she was his lady, and he knew he should be the one to take care of her. He wanted to spoil her rotten. He loved her more and more every day. He hadn't had the chance to sex her since that time at the hotel, but with her moving into her own set, he knew it was going to be on and popping.

When Desiree told him about the apartment, he convinced her to go over at that moment. Once they arrived, they spoke with the owner who lived on the first floor. It was a newly built two-family house with a two-car garage, a balcony, and the whole nine. It was a two-bedroom with two bathrooms, one of which was in the master bedroom, and a den.

He was impressed with her taste. He asked the owner how much he was charging for rent. It was twelve hundred dollars a month, but the owner said he told Desiree she could have it for a thousand. He thought she would be a good tenant. Ishmael saw how he thought that. The way he smiled when talking to her showed him what homeboy was thinking. Ishmael made it known to the man that they were a couple and they would be taking the apartment together.

Ishmael went into his pocket and peeled off 3 g's and gave it to the man on the spot. The owner's eyes lit up. The man rushed into the house and came back with the keys.

On the way back to Beverly's house, Desiree thanked Ishmael and told him she would use her own money to buy some furniture and that she didn't want a dime of his money to do it.

He was cool with that just as long as she was finally going to have her own place and he had somewhere to chill with her.

After kicking it with Derrick for a few hours, Ishmael was grooving. Shit was flowing lovely, and there were no beefs with anyone. They smoked about four blunts between the two of them, and Ishmael drank three shots of Hennessy.

He cruised up the street with his seat leaned way back and his fitted cap pulled over his eyes, bopping his head to the music. He checked up on his blocks and headed home.

While he was driving, he noticed someone tailing him. He made a left at the next block and the car tailing him did the same. He made a right and a quick left at the next two blocks and the other car did the same.

"What the fuck?" he said.

He reached into the console and pushed the button for the trap. He reached in and grabbed his nine and placed it on his lap. He got caught by a red light and thought about running it when he saw the police squatting in the car wash on the other corner. He kept his eyes on the car approaching him. It pulled around to his side of the truck. His window was halfway open, so he rolled it all the way down. He gripped the hammer and sat the nose of the gun on the windowsill.

When the Cadillac pulled up on the side of him, he realized it was Leroy who had several different cars, all of them Cadillacs in different colors. Leroy's driver pulled the Caddy up so that the back window was lined up with Ishmael's. He held the nine in place, not knowing what Leroy was up to.

The back passenger window lowered.

"What's up, Ishmael?" Leroy asked.

"What's up?" Ishmael asked, clearly showing irritation.

"I need to talk to you for a minute."

"About what?"

"Stop by my office," Leroy instructed.

"Naw. Meet me at Hilal's in a half hour," Ishmael said, pulling off, not waiting for a response.

He figured Leroy must have heard about the meeting that he was not invited to. He must know what went down and now he wanted in. Ishmael had other plans, and Leroy could kiss his ass for all he cared. Even though he felt Leroy did him dirty, he still felt some kind of love and respect for the man who helped raise him and school him to the game. But he would never show him that love again.

Ishmael purposely walked into the Hilal restaurant thirty minutes late. In fact he was there before Leroy. He watched him and his bodyguard walk into the restaurant. He stayed in his Benz, which he had gone home and gotten after he pulled off from talking to Leroy. He sat in his car and checked out the scene to see if it was a set-up. Once he was satisfied that it was legit, he shoved his nine down the front of his jeans and went into the restaurant.

Leroy was seated in a booth in the rear. His bodyguard was sitting at the counter. Ishmael walked toward the bodyguard and nodded. The bodyguard got up off the stool and stepped in front of him. He patted Ishmael on the waist.

"What's this?" he whispered in a burly voice.

"What the fuck you think it is?" Ishmael asked, irritated.

"Why you carrying in here?"

"Nigga, I always carry heat. Yo, Leroy." He looked toward the booth where Leroy sat. "What's up wit' yo' boy?"

Leroy waved a hand to the bodyguard. Ishmael threw him prisms as he walked by.

"I don't sit with my back to the door," Ishmael stated, standing in front of Leroy.

"No problem, son. I see I taught you well. Let's sit at this table over here. I'll sit with my back to the door because I got somebody watching my back," he said, laughing.

Ishmael didn't see the humor, so Leroy cleared his throat and sat down in the chair.

Ishmael sat down. Before Leroy could say a word, a tall, dark-skinned woman with a head wrap came over to the table.

"Can I get you brothers anything?" she asked.

"I'll take a sweet tea and a piece of bean pie," Leroy said. He turned to Ishmael. "What do you want, son?"

"Nothing. I'm good," Ishmael said, never taking his eyes off Leroy.

He was pissed at Leroy. Not only for what he did to him, but because his high was now blown fucking around with him.

"So how you been, son?"

"Man, cut the shit. What's up?"

"I wanted to talk to you about the offer again. Youngblood, listen, you're like family to me. I can't sit back and watch you throw your life away."

"You know what, Leroy? That almost sounds sincere, but I ain't feeling it now."

"Ishmael, if you want, you don't have to pay me the ten percent, just give them their fifteen percent and be done with it. Now that's lower than anybody else is paying."

"Maybe if you would've came at me like that earlier, I would still have respect for you, but you didn't. You straight turned your back on me before giving me a chance. And you call yourself being like a father to me. I gave more respect to my real father, and I hated his black ass." Ishmael stood and walked up on the side of Leroy.

His bodyguard got up off the stool and began to walk toward the table.

Ishmael leaned over, "At least he was straight up no matter how fucked up he was, and I respect any man who keeps it real. Stay the fuck away from me."

Just as Ishmael began to walk away, he met Leroy's bodyguard face to face.

"What?" Ishmael shouted, toeing up with the big, burly man.

"Ishmael," Leroy called out to him. Leroy waved to the bodyguard to let Ishmael by.

"I thought so," Ishmael spat at the bodyguard as he walked out.

CHAPTER 40

WHAT IS THE 411

Zola and Nettie were driving in Nettie's car. They pulled up in front of Beverly's house. Beverly was sitting in her usual spot on the porch, holding her bottle of happy juice. The women approached the porch.

"What's up, Bev?" Nettie asked.

"Who dat?" Beverly asked.

She was wasted, and she rocked back and forth, barely able to keep her bloodshot eyes open.

"It's me—Nettie."

"Who?"

"Me Nettie, Bev," Nettie said.

"Who that black bitch with you?" Beverly drawled.

"What?" Zola inquired, stepping forward.

Nettie grabbed her arm and advised her to relax.

"Bev, you wasted. What you drinking?" Nettie asked her, walking a little closer.

"None of your business."

Once Nettie got closer, Beverly began to squint, trying to place her face.

"Oh, what's up, Nettie?" She smiled. "I ain't know who you was." She struggled to talk.

"I figured you didn't. What's good?"

"Ain't nothing, just getting my drink on."

"I know that's right." Nettie sat down on the stoop. "So what's the goings-on in the hood, Bev?"

Zola stood back and looked at Beverly. She wasn't feeling the way Beverly stared at her. And who the hell was she calling a black bitch?

"Ain't nothing going on."

"Come on, Bev, you the four-one-one of the hood. I know you know something."

"What you want to know? You ain't said shit yet," Beverly continued to drawl.

"Bev, I heard there's a new chick in town with green eyes. You know her?"

Beverly took another swig of her liquor and smacked her lips. "Let me get a cigarette?" she asked Nettie, holding out her hand.

"I don't smoke, Bev."

"You don't smoke? When you quit smoking?"

Nettie laughed. Beverly was funny to her.

"Bev, I ain't never smoked. Do you know who the girl is?"

"Who?" Beverly asked with her eyes rolling around in her head.

"The chick with the green eyes."

"Who, Rae-Rae?"

"Is that her name? She got green eyes?" Nettie asked her, looking at Zola.

Zola stepped a little closer, eager to hear more.

"Yeah, her name is Desiree, but we call her Rae-Rae. You know her?"

"Naw, but I heard good things about her. You know where I can find her?"

"She used to live with me but she moved. Her and Ishmael got a place together somewhere in Elizabeth."

Zola's heart sank. Her eyes became red like fire. She was ready to explode. Ishmael did play her.

"I been meaning to go and check out they crib, but I ain't get a chance yet. She said they got a fish tank, and Ishmael bought her a puppy and shit." Beverly continued to talk but neither of them was listening to her.

"Bev, when the next time you think you gonna see her?" Nettie asked.

"Hell, I don't know. Why?"

"I told you I heard good things about her, and I wanted to meet her."

"Meet her for what?"

"I was gonna see if she wanted a job. I heard she had it going on, and we need some new girls at the strip joint," Nettie said, reaching.

"She don't need no job. She got a job. She work for IHOP flipping pancakes and shit." Beverly hiccupped.

"Yeah, which one?"

"I don't know, somewhere in Elizabeth. Why, you going over there?"

"Yeah, I might. Why?"

"Bring me some blueberry pancakes back and some beef sausage." She continued to stumble drunkenly over her words.

"A'ight, Bev, I'll do that. Wait right here. I'll be back," Nettie said as she and Zola got into the car.

"Bring me a pack of cigarettes too," Beverly yelled after the car.

CHAPTER 41

STICKY SITUATIONS

It had been two weeks since Ishmael put out the new product. The blocks were jumping. The product had niggaz hurling all over the place. Fiends were bent. He was sending his deliveryman to the connect faster than he could deliver the product. His territories in the south were feeling the effects as well. They said that niggaz were going bananas over the new product. Everybody wanted to be on his team, asking him to put them on board. Everybody wanted a piece of the cake Ishmael and his squad were making.

He hadn't heard anything from Leroy since last seeing him at the restaurant. Desiree was all moved into her new set, and things were lovely. He barely stayed at his own crib. He would only go there to deposit money into his safe and to check on things at the house.

He had run into Zola a couple of times when he went home. They didn't say too much to each other. She would ask for money to pay some bills and he told her he had it all taken care of. In fact he gave Desiree all the money, and she took care of his bills for him. Zola didn't bitch or complain about anything to him, and he was cool with that. He didn't seem to find her odd behavior strange. He was living life lovely. His product was flowing like crazy, and he and Desiree's relationship was doing well.

Little did he know Zola was watching everything he did when he came home. It wasn't unusual because she did that anyway when they were together. When he dumped the money he had in a garbage bag onto the bed, she remained calm. She watched him stack it into the safe and close it up. He'd grab a few pieces of clothing, and he would be out.

Ishmael tried to call Derrick again, but Derrick didn't answer his cell. It was the third time that day he had tried to reach out to him and got no answer. Lately that had been happening a lot. Ishmael knew Derrick was laid up with the new shorty he was talking to, but he still hadn't met her. The couple of times Ishmael inquired about her, Derrick would either change the subject or tell him she wasn't a street girl, and he didn't want her to know what he was into. Ishmael didn't press the issue.

He headed over to Desiree's to spend time with her before she went to work. He smiled to himself just thinking about how happy he was now that she was in his life. With all that was going on, Ishmael didn't have a clue of the calm before the storm.

The paramedics were putting the body bags of two victims in the back of the wagon. Cohen stood by and watched.

"That's the third body in two weeks," he stated to Sergeant Nicholas.

"I know, cap. There was a lot of body parts in those suitcases. Whoever did this made sure they chopped them up well. All we know is that there's two bodies, now are all pieces to both bodies there? That's what we have to try and figure out by DNA, because the heads are missing," he said.

"Fuck!" Cohen shouted, walking away.

Earlier that day, two women were walking the trail exercising in Weequahic Park, when they saw the two huge suitcases lying in the shallow woods. They went over to investigate. They could see the dried blood that had soaked through the suitcase onto the ground underneath them. The stench from the dead bodies was stomach turning. They reported the whereabouts of the suitcases to a policeman who was sitting in his patrol car in the park.

In the suitcases were body parts chopped into small portions. From what the paramedics could make out, it appeared to be two bodies missing the heads. Just last week cops had found the body of Rallo Jennings

in a heavy-duty garbage bag. Rallo was the young boy who had partici-
pated in robbing Ishmael. His head had been decapitated as well. There
was a missing report filed on him, and through DNA it was confirmed to
be his body. The family had to bury the young man without his head,
which was still missing.

Cohen walked into his office, slamming the door behind him. The
officers who sat at their desks looked on with eager eyes. They knew the
captain was pissed about something.

He sat at his desk and threw his hat to the floor in frustration. He
reached in his bottom drawer and pulled out a bottle of bourbon. He took
a deep swig from the bottle and leaned back in his chair.

He had a strong instinct that Ishmael was behind the murders, but he
couldn't prove it. He had nothing solid to pin the bodies on him. He heard
some talk about Rallo having something to do with robbing one of Ishmael's
workers, but that lead to a dead end. Anything that had Ishmael's name
involved pissed him off. He hadn't received any money from him as of yet,
but Bowen told them that he was cooperating.

Something was going on, and Cohen was going to bust his balls to
find out.

CHAPTER 42

COMING CLEAN

Ishmael and Desiree were cuddled up on the sofa watching the old movie *Life* with Eddie Murphy and Martin Lawrence on DVD. Her new puppy sat on her lap while they watched the movie, which had them in good spirits.

Desiree sat up and looked deep into his eyes.

"What's up, baby?" He kissed her on the lips.

"I need to talk to you," she said, setting the puppy on the floor. He went running off into the bedroom.

"Come on, let's talk," he said, giving her his undivided attention.

"You know I'm still having nightmares sometimes," she admitted.

"Yeah, I know. You had one the other night, but I didn't want to wake you."

"Well, I remembered when you said that in order to move on I should talk about my past and get it all out in the open."

"Yeah, I thought you did that."

"No way. There's a whole lot more." She giggled.

"Damn. Okay, shoot."

"Well I'm a recovering addict."

He looked at her like she was crazy.

"No, you're not."

"Yes, I am. I was a free-baser. I smoked rock for a long time. I was a mess." She shook her head.

"I can't believe that," he said, looking at her. "So that's why you don't want to be around it."

"Exactly. That's why I have a problem with you slinging. I promised myself that I wouldn't surround myself with the very same things that got me where I was when I was locked down."

"Yeah, I feel you," he said.

"But there's more."

"Okay," he said, interested at what could be worst than armed robbery, serving time in prison, and being an outright crack head. This woman was full of secrets, he thought.

"When I lived on Fifteenth Avenue, one day I was at home getting high with a good friend of mine. My then boyfriend, Bunchy—you know I told you about him—"

Ishmael nodded. He stared deeply into her unique beautiful green eyes and played with her long hair while she talked.

"Well, he was cutting his friend's hair when some thugs busted the door down to our apartment." She stopped talking and began to twiddle her fingers, fighting back tears.

"Go 'head, baby. You can do it. I'm right here for you."

She took a deep breath and continued, "They busted into the apartment, and the door fell on Bunchy. They shot my friend Tracey. I've never seen anything like that before. They blew off half her face and her arm." The tears began to stream down her face. "They hit Roc in the face with the gun, and he fell out. There wasn't nothing I could do to help them."

Ishmael stared at her blankly while she talked.

"So much was going on that I can't remember every little detail, but I remember the murders clearly. I remember they all were wearing black and had on ski masks. I remember the head gunman grabbing me by my neck, and his breath smelled like violets. That's why I asked you to stop eating the candy, because it reminded me of that day," she said, sniffing.

Ishmael was in a state of shock. He couldn't believe what he was hearing. This couldn't have been the same people he and his crew mirked years earlier. No way it was Desiree. Those were a bunch fiends they ran in on.

"All I kept seeing for a long time afterward was when the dude pointed his gun at Roc's head and pulled the trigger." She lay on his chest and continued to cry, letting all the bottled-up secrets spill out of her eyes.

Ishmael sat in silence, holding her and thinking back on that day. Was that her? Then it hit him like a ton of bricks. Those eyes. It was her. That's where he knew those eyes from. His heart started to beat faster. There was no way in the world he was ever going to let her find out that he killed Roc.

"So now that you know all about my past, do you still want to be with me?" she asked like an innocent child.

"Of course I do, baby. The past is the past, and don't you ever forget that. Anything that happened in the past stays there." He tried to look like nothing was on his mind. In fact he was tripping out on how he hooked up with the very same person who could put him behind bars for life.

They sat on the couch cuddled up until it was time for her to get ready for work. He dropped her off at IHOP and set out in search of Derrick. He couldn't wait to catch up with him and tell him what he found out about Desiree.

CHAPTER 43

MIA

Ishmael drove around town checking on his blocks and asking Derrick's whereabouts. No one had seen him. He tried to reach out to him again on his cell phone and still no answer. He swung by Derrick's crib and his truck wasn't there. There was no answer at the door either. He couldn't figure out where Derrick could be. He checked with Nate, Dice, and Click, but nobody knew anything.

He was scheduled to meet with the deliveryman and security in a couple of hours, so he reached out to Damon to see if he heard anything from Derrick. Most likely he hadn't, but Ishmael figured it was worth a shot.

What's up, Ish?" Damon shouted into the phone.

"What's good? You heard from Rik?"

"Naw, man, I ain't see that nigga in like months and shit," he exaggerated.

"Yeah, a'ight."

"Where you headed?" Damon inquired.

"I'm on my way to the crib. I need to re-up today."

"Oh, a'ight, so what time I need to come through to the drop house?"

"Maybe in about four or five hours, I don't know. I'll hit you when it gets there."

"A'ight, man."

"One!" Ishmael disconnected the call.

Something wasn't right. It had been several days since he talked to Derrick. Now he knew Derrick was sweet on this new bitch he was seeing, but damn. *The bitch must can suck the fuck out of some dick to have this nigga in hibernation,* he thought. Oh well, he needed to take care of business.

The first thing he was going to do was check up on the house and pick up the buy money, then he would drop it off at the stash house with Nate, Dice, and Click. After that, he would check up on Beverly to see if she had heard from or seen Derrick.

Derrick was sitting on the sofa in Nettie's apartment. She was in the kitchen cooking him up a nice meal.

They had been shacked up together for days. He was enjoying himself with her. She was a little freak, and she knew just what to do to him. She was a good cook and kept his belly full. She would give him great massages, and they took long showers together. Derrick was really feeling her, and he wanted to take what they had a step farther. At that point he didn't care what anybody thought about them. She brought him his plate. He set it down on the tray and pulled her close to him. He kissed her deeply. He smacked her hard on the ass as she went to fetch her own plate.

"So I know your boy think you're missing in action," she said, sitting next to him.

"Yeah, he been hitting me up. I'll get with him in a few. Today is pickup day."

"Oh, so y'all go over and pick up weight?" she inquired.

"Naw, we got people to do that. We don't touch no product," he said, shoving a forkful of homemade lasagna in his mouth.

"So y'all just give y'all money to somebody else to go pick up for y'all?"

"Yeah."

"That shit is crazy. What if they beat y'all for the loot?"

"Nett, that ain't gonna never happen," he assured her.

"You can't be trusting niggaz out here like that."

"I been in this shit for a minute. I know what I'm doing."

"Okay. If you say so." She bit a piece of buttered Italian bread. "So let me get this straight, y'all be riding around with a whole lot of paper to pass off to someone else who then goes and picks up and then they bring the product back to y'all?"

"Something like that, except we don't touch the product. It goes to another spot to get cut and bagged. Now can you let me finish eating and watching this game?" He pointed toward the TV.

She sucked her teeth and rolled her eyes at him. He grabbed her arm and pulled her toward him and shoved his tongue in her mouth. She smiled at him, and they continued to eat their meal.

An hour later Derrick was getting the hell sucked out of his tool by Nettie.

Nettie looked up at him while she sucked him off. His face was showing her just how good she was making him feel. But then again the face of every man she sucked off looked like that. She knew she had skills. She was definitely nice with hers, and she had that shit down to a science.

Derrick moaned and groaned while Nettie slurped his juices after he nutted in her mouth. She continued to suck on him like he was a pacifier.

Derrick let out a blood-curdling scream. Nettie sat up and watched him squirm and wiggle as he yelled and cried out. His blood spilled from her mouth and ran down to her chin.

She had sliced the top half of his dick off and spit it to the floor. She wiped her mouth with the back of her hand, got up, and walked around to the side of the bed.

"You bitch," Derrick yelled, gasping for breath.

He held on to his crotch as blood quickly soaked the sheets. He was losing blood by the pound, and it was getting hard for him to breathe.

Nettie removed the blade from her mouth and grabbed Derrick by his dreads. She held his head back, exposing his neck. He grabbed her arm with force, almost throwing her to the floor. She quickly regained her balance, and she pounced on him like a black cat.

Before Derrick realized it, Nettie had slit his throat from ear to ear. Her work was done.

CHAPTER 44

SNATCHED

Security had just left the stash house.

"A'ight, something stinks," Ishmael said to the members who were in attendance.

"Rik didn't show up for the pickup. On the real, something's up. Are y'all sure none of y'all has seen or heard from him?" he asked.

They all agreed that none of them had seen him.

"Check it, I want all of y'all to hit the streets and find out whatever you can. I don't care if you have to yoke a few mafuckas up to get word, do it." His gut was working overtime. He knew something had happened to Derrick, but he didn't know what or even who. Derrick was not a dude who could be easily taken down. He knew there wasn't any way a bitch had Derrick hemmed up for that amount of time.

They all filed out of the stash house on a mission. Ishmael sat there a while longer then he left. He drove around aimlessly, looking for his friend. He checked the time, and it was 3:00 A.M. Desiree would be getting off work in four hours. He figured he would swing by, pick her up, and drop her off at home, then hit the streets again.

He was tired. He didn't get much sleep the night before. Since Desiree didn't have to work, they had a fuck session like no other. He had left that morning to run errands, and he stopped by the braid shop to get his hair done. Once he'd done all his running around, he was back with Desiree, watching a movie until it was time for her to go to work.

He thought again about what she had told him earlier. It was freaking him out that she was actually in the house when it all went down. This world was definitely too small. You never knew who was who.

While Ishmael drove around stressing out about Desiree and Derrick, he never noticed that he'd been followed for the last hour.

It was 4:05 A.M., and there was no sign of Ishmael. Desiree had called him at 3:30 on his cell phone and told him to pick her up. She had a headache, and her supervisor was letting her leave early. Desiree walked to the corner and looked around for him. It was cold and the wind blowing seemed to make her head hurt worst. She was getting a little frustrated because it was the third time that month he had been late to pick her up. She was grateful to have a ride, but she was tired and her head was killing her. She made a mental note to remember to talk to him about having her wait on him. She was his lady, and she should come first. This was exactly why she didn't want to depend on anyone. She'd rather do things for herself.

The morning was quiet, and the birds began to chirp. She looked up the street in both directions, searching for any sign of him. She noticed a man with a large Afro and sunglasses heading toward her. She began to feel uncomfortable so she decided to go back inside and wait for Ishmael. Her face and ears were cold so going back inside the restaurant was a good idea. As she walked up to the restaurant, a black van pulled up in front of her.

It all happened so fast. The man walking toward her bum-rushed her, and the van doors opened. He put his hand over her mouth and shoved her. She didn't go willingly so a man inside the van grabbed her arms and pulled her in.

The man inside the van was wearing a ski mask, and the driver who appeared to be a female also wore an afro wig with sunglasses.

She tried to fight the two men in the back of the van, but they slapped her several times across the face, causing her severe pain. She just lay still, hoping they would stop beating her.

They blindfolded and gagged her and tied her hands and feet. She lay on the cold, hard metal floor of the old van. She was terrified. Tears ran down her face fast and hard. She began to think about the day Roc and Tracey were murdered. She escaped with her life that day. For some reason, Desiree knew she wouldn't escape this day. No one was that lucky.

Ishmael raced through the streets like a bat out of hell, heading to pick Desiree up from work. He was so stressed he lost track of time. The product had gotten dropped off to get bagged. When he tried to call Damon to go to the drop house, Damon didn't answer his cell.

"What the fuck is going on?" he said.

He flew up the street in his whip. He pulled into the parking lot of the restaurant like a bat out of hell. He sat and waited in the truck for Desiree to come outside. He continued to think about Derrick. He made a few phones call to the crew, and the status was still the same. No one had heard anything from Derrick. He called Damon. There was no answer.

"Damn. Everybody's missing," he said out loud. "Where the hell is she?" He looked toward the restaurant.

He had things he needed to do, and Desiree had him sitting in the parking lot waiting on her. He jumped out of the truck and went inside the restaurant. Hazel the manager saw him come in and went over to him.

"What can I do for you, boyfriend?" she flirted.

Ishmael was not in the mood for Hazel's Stella-got-her-groove-back antics.

"Hey, Hazel. Where's Rae?"

"She left. I thought she forgot something and you was coming in for her because of the migraine she had." She looked at him, puzzled.

"No she ain't with me. I just got here. She called me, but I was running a little late."

Now he was confused. Where could she be?

"Well all I know is she called you, and she went outside to wait for you. Maybe she got tired of waiting and caught a cab home, or maybe she called another ride."

"A'ight. Thanks, Hazel," he said, not wasting anymore time talking to her. *That can't be possible. Desiree doesn't know anybody else who she could call to come get her. Maybe she got tired of waiting and did catch a cab home,* he thought. This pissed him off, because he had tried several times to convince her into letting him purchase her a car. But no, she didn't want him to buy it. She wouldn't even let him get her a cell phone. He was fed up with the I-don't-need-no-man-to-do-for-me women liberation shit. He was going to get her cell phone, and there wasn't shit she was going to do but take it. He was the man not her.

Ishmael continued to argue with himself in his head as he drove. He stopped by the house.

"Rae," he called out to her once he was inside.

There was no answer. She wasn't there yet. The puppy ran and bit the bottom of his jeans, playfully tugging and pulling on him. He was not in the mood to play so he kicked the puppy who ran off yelping and hid under the sofa.

Ishmael sat on the sofa when his cell phone began to ring.

"Yeah," he said.

"Hey, boo."

"Who dis?" he asked with a frown on his face.

"Oh, so you don't know my voice anymore?" It was Zola.

"What you want, Zo?" he asked, irritated.

"What are you doing?"

"What do you want, Zola?" he repeated.

"I was just wondering if you're coming home tonight."

"Have I been coming home?" he asked sarcastically.

"No."

"A'ight then. Is that all you want?" He didn't feel like playing games. He had enough going on.

"I guess so."

"One!" He disconnected the call and turned on the television.

CHAPTER 45

TIME RUNNING OUT

Desiree sat blindfolded and tied to a chair in an abandoned house. Two candles sat on the floor in the corner next to her, dimly lighting the room. She could hear squeaking as mice ran around the room. She was cold and terrified. She could hardly breathe because of the stench of urine. She tried to break free of the ropes that were wrapped around her wrists, body, and legs. She couldn't break free, so she began to cry.

She heard the door to the room open. She could hear several footsteps but no one talked. She could feel them staring at her, and this frightened her more.

"So what you wanna do with this green-eyed bitch?" a female voice said with jealousy, finally breaking the silence.

"First, I'm gonna plug every hole in her pretty ass, then we gonna put her outta her misery," a male stated.

"*Ilk!*" the female said.

"Ay, hold up, you ain't say nothing 'bout mirking this broad," another male voice said.

Desiree was freaking out because she knew she was going to die. She began to scream the best she could. She squirmed, trying to break free.

"Look at this bitch. She feisty as hell, just like I like 'em," the first male stated.

"You a sick bastard," the female shouted.

"Man, let's just go get this loot, and you can do whatever you want to the broad. I ain't with that sick shit you into," the other male stated.

Desiree didn't recognize any of the voices. She wished Ishmael was there to save her.

"A'ight, let's do this," one of the males said. "I'll be back for you, shorty." He touched her face.

Desiree began to scream. The female punched Desiree in her face with all her might. Desiree belted out a loud grunt. The pain was unbearable.

"Backstabbing bitch," the female yelled.

"A'ight, chill. Let's be out," one of the men said, and they walked out of the room.

Twenty minutes later at Ishmael's house, Damon, Zola, and Niles pulled up into the driveway.

Damon had convinced Niles to get down with them on robbing Ishmael. After Ishmael told Damon to watch out for Niles the day he came home from the joint, Damon stuck to him like glue. He realized Niles was an a'ight dude, so the two became tight. Damon told Niles all about how Ishmael didn't trust him anymore and thought he was a rat. Niles was pissed because he looked up to Ishmael. The charge he took was for Ishmael who told him to take it because he was a minor and it would be his first charge, so he wouldn't get that much time. He was loyal to Ishmael so he did it. Ishmael did take care of him while he was locked up, but that was still no reason to kick dirt on Niles. So after Damon came to him about Ishmael, he was down for the payback.

They all exited the vehicle. Zola took out her keys, and they walked into the house.

Parked in a black Lincoln with limousine-tinted windows was Arnold Bowen and the hit man. Bowen looked around suspiciously. Ten minutes later, Bowen and the hit man got out of the vehicle.

They crept up to the front of the house. The door was locked. The hit man took out some tools to pick a lock. Several minutes later, he got the lock open. Bowen removed his .380 and they went inside.

Cohen was sitting several houses away in a different direction watching the whole thing. He was squatting on Ishmael. He had been staking out his house for several days, trying to get anything on him to connect him to the murders. Cohen got out of his car, heading over to the house.

Inside of the house the three stood inside the closet looking at the safe. Niles was squatting in front of it playing with the dials.

"You think you can get it open?" Zola asked.

"I think I can." He studied the safe closely. "Ish didn't spare no paper when he copped this." He admired the heavy armor on the safe.

"Hurry up and crack that mafucka," Damon said, losing patience.

Niles was an ex-burglar until Ishmael put him onto the world of hustling. Before then he could pretty much figure out any system to get what he wanted, and safes were his pet peeve. He loved the challenge they offered.

"Hurry the fuck up, man," Damon pushed.

"Chill, D. We got time. Ishmael ain't coming home tonight," Zola assured him.

"Did that blade-sucking bitch take care of Rik?" he grilled her.

She looked at him like he had lost his mind and rolled her eyes at him.

"You don't hear me talking to you?" he shouted.

"Yeah, mafucka. Damn. Rik is a memory," she shouted back.

"Yo, y'all niggaz shut the fuck up. I'm tryna concentrate on this mafucka, and y'all standing here beefin'!" Niles looked over his shoulder at the two of them.

Damon had no patience, so he walked out of the closet. "Yo, anything in this mafucka to eat?" he stopped and asked Zola.

"I don't know. Check in the kitchen," she said, irritated with him.

"You live in this bitch, and you don't know what's here to eat?" he said, walking out of the room.

Damon went down to the kitchen and stuck his head into the refrigerator, trying to find something to munch on. He thought he heard a noise and snatched his .40, ready to let off. He looked out into the dining room and listened for a minute, then he placed the gun back in the waistband of his jeans and continued to search the icebox.

Niles was in complete concentration trying to open the safe. Zola thought getting something to eat was a good idea.

"Niles, I'm going to see what this bum is doing. You want something to eat?"

"No," he shouted, irritated because of the interruption.

"A'ight, damn." She stormed out of the room.

She went downstairs and walked into the kitchen. Damon was making himself a turkey-and-cheese sandwich.

"What you doing down here?" he asked, taking a big bite out of his sandwich.

"I'm getting me something to eat too." She pushed past him.

Zola began to make herself a sandwich as well. Damon leaned up against the counter and watched her while he ate.

Zola's cell phone started to ring. It was Nettie.

"Hey. What's up, Nett?"

"Did you get the loot yet?" Nettie asked.

"No, not yet. Slow-ass Niles is tryna get the safe open now."

"So where you want to meet at when you get it?" Nettie questioned.

"Oh, you can meet us at the abandoned house on Twelfth Avenue. That's where we got the green-eyed bitch stashed at," she said.

"What the fuck is you doing?" Damon yelled.

"What?"

"Why you telling ha that shit over the phone?"

"What are you talking about, D?"

"You telling Nettie that we got Rae-Rae stashed on Twelfth Avenue. Hang up the damn phone. Five-O could have your phone tapped."

She sucked her teeth at him. "Nett, this buster acting all paranoid and shit. I'll call you when we get it." She disconnected the call. "Happy?" She looked at him.

"You's a dumb bitch," he projected.

Damon felt a pinch in the side of his neck. When he touched it, there was a dart sticking out of it. He pulled out the dart and looked at it.

"What the fuh?" he contemplated, studying the dart.

Suddenly his vision became blurred, and he tried to grab onto the countertop for balance. He slid down and fell to his death onto the kitchen floor. Zola looked at him and thought he was playing.

"D," she said, kicking his leg, "get up."

He didn't move.

"Damon! What's wrong with you?"

He still didn't move. She saw the dart lying on the floor next to him.

She picked it up and looked at it strangely.

She ran out of the kitchen to tell Niles what was going on. Out of the corner of her eye she saw a shadow. She knew someone was in the house, and she began to panic. She screamed and tried to run up the stairs. The hit man pulled a hunting knife from its holster and threw it at her. The knife planted itself in the back of her head. She tumbled backward down the stairs. The hit man waved to Bowen to come out of hiding. He held up two fingers, letting Bowen know that that was two down and one to go.

The two men began to climb the stairs.

"Freeze," Cohen said, bursting into the front door.

CHAPTER 46

CAUGHT

Upstairs Niles heard the commotion downstairs, and his street instinct kicked in. He grabbed his tools off the floor and headed for the window. He shimmied down the fire escape and jumped to the ground. Niles took off running through the neighborhood backyards.

"Hey, Arnie boy, what we got here?" Cohen asked with a wide smile.

The hit man looked at Bowen like he had been set up. Bowen looked at Cohen like he had seen a ghost.

How does he keep finding out? he wondered.

"Hey, is this the same guy you got to do the other job?" Cohen pointed at the hit man. "Wow, you're still in business, huh? How much does that job pay? I was thinking about changing my occupation."

"Bobby, what are you doing here?" Bowen asked.

"Well, I was waiting for the owner of this really nice house," Cohen said, looking around and realizing how laid the crib was. "I think I might just go into the drug business instead." He stroked the Italian furniture.

The hit man began to inch backward when Cohen sensed him trying to escape.

"Hold on there, buddy. Going somewhere?" Cohen moved forward, pointing his .40 Glock at him.

"Come on, Bobby. Give me break here," Bowen pleaded.

"You've been a naughty boy, Arnie."

Cohen walked cautiously toward the two men.

"Don't move," he told the hit man. "Well, well, well, I see we got us a double homicide, Arnie." He looked at the two bodies.

"Ay, come on, Bobby." Bowen held out his hands, still holding the gun.

"Whoa, dropped the gun, buddy."

Bowen placed the gun on the shiny hardwood floor while holding his other hand up.

"Now kick it over here," Cohen instructed.

Bowen did as he was told. The gun whisked across the floor, spinning, and finally coming to a stop at Cohen's feet. He picked up the gun.

"What are you doing, Bobby? Hey, man, we can do just like before. What percentage do you want?" Bowen smiled nervously.

The hit man eyed the two men as they talked.

"There were three of them. Where's the other one? Did you off him too?" Cohen asked.

"No. We don't know where he is. We were going to see if he was upstairs," Bowen said, panting.

"Well, let's just go find out where he is. After you, gentlemen." Cohen smiled.

The closer he got, the more Bowen could smell the Bourbon that seeped through his pores.

Bowen turned to go up the stairs first.

"After you," Cohen said to the hit man.

Like a thief in the night, the hit man spun around and grabbed Cohen's hand that held the gun. He twisted his arm so that the gun was positioned right in his stomach. Before Cohen knew what hit him, he placed his finger around Cohen's and pumped the lead into his belly until the clip was empty, then he grabbed Bowen's gun, which had fallen to the floor and pointed it at Bowen.

"What are you doing?" Bowen asked with his hands in the air.

"You set me up," the hit man said in demonic tone.

"No I didn't," Bowen said, pissing in his pants.

"How does this man keep finding out what we're doing?"

"I don't know, but I swear I didn't set you up," Bowen continued to plead.

The hit man fired off three shots into Bowen's chest. He fell to the floor lying next to Cohen. He placed the gun next to Bowen, stripped off his gloves, stuffed them in his pocket, and left the house.

Niles was standing at a pay phone. His heart was racing. He didn't know what to do. He was calling Ishmael to get help. He knew what would happen if Ishmael found out that he tried to rob him and set him up, so he decided to rat out Zola and Damon.

"Who dis?" Ishmael asked.

"It's me Niles, man."

"What's up? Where all y'all niggaz at? I called the drop house and everybody is there but you and D. I can't get in touch with Rik. What the fuck is going on?" he shouted, vexed.

"Ishmael man, I need to see you like yesterday. Damon did some foul shit, and I just found out about it."

"What?"

"Man, just come get me. I don't want to tell you over this box. It might be tapped."

Niles told Ishmael where he was. Ishmael turned off the TV and jetted out the door. He jumped into his truck and peeled off, tires screeching up the street. The car that sat on the corner pulled out behind him.

Ishmael's mind was racing just as fast as he drove his whip through the streets. He ran several red lights in the process. Desiree didn't show up at the house. He had no way of contacting her and didn't know if something had happened to her. He decided to make a phone call back to the crib and leave her a message just in case she came home while he was gone. After placing the call, he tried Derrick's cell phone again. This time someone picked up the line but there was silence.

"Hello? Hello?" he shouted into the phone. "Rik?"

The line went dead, so he redialed the number, and the voice mail automatically came on.

"What the fuck is going on?" he shouted.

Ishmael was losing his cool, which was something he never did.

He pulled up to the corner where Niles instructed him to pick him up, but he wasn't there. Ishmael looked around and didn't see him. The vehicle that was following him was sitting three blocks back with the headlights turned off.

Ishmael began to drive off when he heard Niles shout out his name. He slammed on the brakes and backed up. Niles appeared from behind a building and ran low to the ground and jumped into the truck. Once inside, he laid the seat all the way back.

"Fuck is up with you?" Ishmael asked, confused, pulling off from the curb.

"Man, shit is hectic out here."

"What?" Ishmael shouted, tired of all the trivia.

"Man, your boy D…I found out he did some fucked-up shit."

"I don't have time for the bullshit."

"Ish, I heard D and Zola talking. They didn't know I was listening, but they said that they was going to yo' crib and rob the safe," Niles said, trying to sound convincing so Ishmael wouldn't know he was part of the scheme and go bonkers on his ass.

"What?" Ishmael looked at him. "I'ma go over there. They there now? That grimy bitch. I knew I should have cancelled her ass."

"Naw, man, don't go there. I followed them over to yo' crib, and I think five-O got 'em. The cops rolled up to your crib like ten deep, so I hauled ass," Nile exaggerated.

"Word?"

"Word, man."

"Shit," Ishmael retorted.

"That ain't it, Ish." Niles looked scared.

Ishmael looked at him with evil eyes. He was so pissed that the veins in his neck were bulging.

"Ish, they kidnapped your girl," he said, closing his eyes, waiting for the explosion.

"What?" Ishmael yelled, slamming on the brakes, coming to a screeching halt. "Fuck is you talking about?"

"Man, I heard them say that shit. I don't know, man," Niles stuttered.

"Why the fuck didn't you say that shit from the rip? I don't give a fuck about no paper. My girl is more important than that," he yelled, snatching the boy up.

"Ish! I know, man, but I'm scared. All them cops at your crib got me spooked."

Ishmael let him go. He looked at Niles with unsure eyes.

"Where she at?" he asked calmly.

"I'll show you. Make a left at the corner." Niles pointed, never taking his eyes off Ishmael.

CHAPTER 47

THE SPOT

"Park over here." Niles had Ishmael park two houses down from the abandoned property. Ishmael looked over at Niles as he turned off the vehicle. Niles looked at him then quickly turned away. They got out of the truck and walked toward the abandoned house.

They walked around the back. Ishmael pulled out his hammer, ready to let off. Niles pulled the board that was covering the door to the side. He squeezed in, and Ishmael followed.

It was pitch black in the house. Up ahead, light was seeping through the doorjamb of a room. Ishmael tripped over whatever was on the floor several times while Niles knew where to step, avoiding the trash.

Niles opened the door and walked inside with Ishmael on his tail. When Ishmael looked at Desiree, his heart sank. She was dirty, and her hair was all over her head. He was ready to cry at the sight of his true love.

"Aw damn, baby." He ran over to her.

When Desiree heard his voice, she began to cry and scream through the bandana that was over her mouth. Ishmael kissed her face and pulled off the bandana. He removed the blindfold from her eyes.

"Oh, baby." He kissed her deeply.

She cried and kissed her man, happy to see him. He began to try and loosen the ropes.

"Ishmael, what is going on?" she questioned.

"I don't know, baby, but please believe somebody gonna pay for this shit."

"Why did they do this to me? Are you in some trouble?" She continued to cry.

"No, baby, I'm not in any trouble." He struggled with the ropes.

Ishmael removed his pocketknife and began to cut the ropes. Once Desiree was free, she leaped into his arms, and they embraced passionately.

"Rae, I need you to be straight with me, baby. Did you see any faces?"

"I barely saw their faces. They had on disguises. Ishmael, who would do something like this to me?" she asked, looking into his eyes.

He held his head low. "Rae, it was Zola, my ex, and D, one of my boys."

"Your ex? Why would she want to kill me?"

"Rae, she's a crazy bitch. That's why I cut her loose."

"And this other guy was supposed to be your boy?"

"Yeah exactly, supposed to be," he agreed. "Rae, there is so much going on, and I can't figure none of it out. My boy Rik is missing." He shook his head.

"But Ishmael, you mentioned two people, and there were three—two guys and one female." Desiree looked puzzled.

"Three?" he asked her, confused.

"Yeah. I'm sure there were three."

"You sure, baby, because my man Niles over there told me it was Damon and Zola."

They both looked at each other then at Niles who was leaning against the wall in deep thought. Ishmael stood and pointed his hammer at Niles.

"Ishmael, no. What are you doing? He brought you here to save me," Desiree screamed, pulling his arm.

This broke Niles out of his thoughts and made him aware that Ishmael was pointing his gun at him.

"You's a punk-ass nigga," Ishmael growled.

"Ish, what's up, man?" Niles stuttered, ready to shit his pants.

"You tell me, nigga."

"Yo, man, I didn't do anything," Niles said, panicking.

"Oh yeah?"

"Yeah, man, it wasn't me. How you know Rik ain't have nothing to do with this? He's the one missing," Niles retorted.

Ishmael stood there contemplating what Niles just said. No, his boy wouldn't do that to him. They were boys. But where was he? He'd been MIA for days now. He never returned any of his calls. Ishmael hated to think that his boy would do something like that to him. He had no reason, but then again maybe he wanted his spot. It happened all the time.

While he thought about what Niles had said, Desiree was staring at Niles with wide eyes as if she had seen a ghost.

"Oh my God," Desiree said with her hand to her mouth.

"What is, baby?" Ishmael asked.

"That voice. He was one of them," she screamed.

"What?" Ishmael looked back at her.

"She lying, Ish. I didn't have shit to do with it." Niles stumbled over his words.

Something didn't smell right, and it was Niles.

"You calling my girl a liar?" Ishmael moved closer to Niles, still pointing the hammer at him.

"No, Ish!" Niles began to cry.

"Don't bitch up now, nigga. You gonna wear this one," he growled.

Ishmael's eyes appeared to glow in the dark, and Niles began to plead and beg for his life.

"Ishmael baby, don't do this," Desiree tried to reason. "He ain't worth it. I'm alright now. Let's just call the police."

But Ishmael wasn't hearing her. He had transformed.

"You want to fuck me and mine? Nigga, you don't know by now not to fuck with me?" Ishmael's voice had changed; he was another person. He was anyone's worst nightmare.

Desiree stood there looking at the man she loved and didn't recognize him. This odd behavior sent chills through her body. She knew he was going to kill the boy, and there was nothing she could do about it. She didn't want Niles to lose his life although earlier she feared she was going to lose hers. She did remember when he said he didn't want to have anything to do with killing her, so she felt his life should be spared. She just wanted to get out of the scary house, but Ishmael was another person, and she dared not try to stop him. He might turn the gun on her.

Niles was crying like a baby. Snot was running out his nose and slob fell from his bottom lip. He continued to plead and beg, but Ishmael didn't hear him.

Ishmael was calm but he looked dangerously deranged. He stood there glaring at Niles with cold eyes.

"Ishmael, please, I would never do anything to hurt your girl, please." He made a last attempt.

Ishmael pointed the gun directly at his head. With a smile, he shouted, "See you in hell, baby" before he pulled the trigger.

He shot Niles in the head, and when his body fell to the floor, he pumped two more into his chest.

Desiree was in shock. She began to cry, and her entire body shook. He turned and looked at her.

"You a'ight, baby?" he asked as if he didn't just murder a man at point-blank range.

He began to walk toward her. She backed up and almost fell over the chair that was behind her.

"Get away from me," she yelled.

"Baby, what's wrong?" he asked, stopping in his tracks.

"Get the fuck away from me, you murderer," she cried.

"Rae, that mafucka was gonna to kill you. I'll do anything for you," he tried to convince her.

"You bastard!" She could barely breathe. "You killed my friends!" She coughed.

"Rae, what are you talking about?" He stepped closer to her.

"It was you. It all makes sense now. The violet candy…I remember now." She began moving closer to the door to get away from him. "It was you. You killed Tracey and Roc."

When he said those words—"See you in hell, baby"—that horrible day came back to her. She remembered him saying those exact words before killing Roc. She remembered smelling the violets on his breath.

"Come on, baby. You're just scared right now. Listen to what you're saying. Come here." He tried to comfort her.

How the fuck did she know? What did he do to let her know it was him who killed her friends? He had to convince her otherwise. He just couldn't lose another love, he argued with himself in his head.

"Baby, how could I have killed your friends? Think about it. I

"Let her go, Carlos. She don't have shit to do with this. This is between me and you," Ishmael stated. He couldn't believe he was staring at his ex-girlfriend Sasha's brother.

Ishmael and Sasha were in love. He loved everything about her and everything she stood for. He had met her through her brother Carlos. They both were in the business together. Ishmael got his product from Carlos who did all the work for his father Vinnie who was a big man in New York. The two of them became close, and he ended up meeting Sasha at a family dinner.

One night Carlos told Ishmael that he didn't think it would be a good idea to date his sister anymore, but Ishmael had gotten the approval from their father who treated him like a son, and he ignored his friend's request.

Leroy and Vinnie were rivals. When Leroy found out that Ishmael was no longer getting his goods from his supplier, he was pissed off because Ishmael was his main purchaser. Leroy was jealous that Ishmael was closer to Vinnie, so Leroy started some shit with Vinnie unbeknownst to Ishmael.

Carlos and Vinnie changed their behavior toward him because they thought he was trying to set them up. They told him never to see Sasha again.

Ishmael was hurt. He couldn't understand what happened, and to this day he still didn't know what happened. He killed Sasha, but he had no other choice. Vinnie and Carlos had brainwashed her into thinking that he was the devil.

After the breakup, three months later Ishmael got a call from Sasha. She wanted him to meet her at a hotel in Manhattan. Ishmael was happy to hear from her. He missed her so much and wanted nothing in the world than to convince her he didn't do the things her father and brother told her.

He showed up to the hotel and was greeted by a beautiful yet sensual Sasha. They made love for what he now knew as their last time. He talked to her and tried to convince her to move away with him. He was ready to give up the game to spend the rest of his life with her.

The door came flying open and in walked Carlos and his two goons.

"What's going on? *Como esta?*" Ishmael looked at Sasha for an answer.

She lowered her head, showing him that she knew.

He was hurt, he couldn't believe she would set him up. He loved her.

"Yeah, papi it's your time," Carlos stated. "Madi, move out of the way," he instructed her. *"Bein na ca!"*

Ishmael thought about reaching for his gat that was under the pillow on the bed, but he knew he wouldn't be fast enough.

Out of nowhere Leroy's muscle came in through the door blazin'. It was chaos. Bullets where flying everywhere. Ishmael reached under the pillow for his gat and dove to the floor.

When the smoke cleared Carlos and his goons where dead—or so he thought. Ishmael stood there in his boxers and looked at the bloody men lying on the floor. He thought about Sasha and looked around for her, but she wasn't there. Then he saw the bathroom door closed and knocked on the door.

"Sash, are you in there?"

"Ishmael, is it over?" she asked, sounding like an innocent child.

"Yeah, baby, come on out."

"Is Carlito okay?"

Ishmael looked at Carlos and lowered his head, "No, baby, he's gone. *Bein.*"

He stepped back at the sound of the door opening. To his surprise Sasha was crying, and she held a .22 in her hand, pointing at Ishmael.

"What are you doing, baby?" he asked, shocked.

He heard Leroy's men click the chambers of their weapons. He held his hand up to advise them to hold on.

"Sasha, give me the gun." He held his hand out to her.

"You killed Carlito," she cried, looking at her brother lying on the floor in a pool of blood. "You said you loved me."

"I do love you, baby."

"You don't like me poppa either. You want to kill my whole family, Ishmael," she continued to cry. *"Oh aye dios mejo!"* she spoke in Spanish.

"Don't look at them, baby. Just give me the gun."

Pop!

Sasha shot him in the shoulder. Ishmael grabbed his shoulder.

"No," he screamed at the men. He knew that it was only a matter of seconds before they would turn her into Swiss cheese.

"Sasha, think about what you're doing. Baby, I love you. Just give me the gun."

He looked into her eyes and saw a different person. This was a woman who believed he was out to kill her and her family. Her brother was already dead, and she feared for her own life.

"What you gonna do, Ishmael?" one of the security men yelled, scaring the life out of Sasha.

That caused her to let off another shot. This one missed him.

He had to make a choice, and his choice was between his life or hers. He loved her, but he knew because of her family's status he would never be able to be with her again.

He raised his gun in one movement and popped her in her dome. He watched her drop to the floor. He stood there for a few minutes, but he was snatched up by the men, and they fled the hotel down the back staircase.

"Listen, Carlos, I had nothing to do with whatever beef your father had. I was your boy. I would never try to set you and your family up."

"Too late, homey. I had to have five operations to remove all the bullets. It took me a year to be able to walk again. I got a metal plate in my head and a bullet lodged next to my spine. They can't remove it, fearing that I may be paralyzed for life."

"Let my lady go, man," Ishmael requested.

"I been watching you for over three years, tryna figure out how I was going to get revenge. I could have popped you long ago, but I wanted you to suffer like me." Carlos smiled.

"I didn't do anything to you," Ishmael yelled, frustrated.

"How do I know that? A son will do anything for his father. I did for mine, so I know you would for yours."

"What are you talking about? My father is dead, man."

"No, Ishmael, your father is very much alive." He smiled.

"What are you talking about?"

The door to the room flew open, brightened by beams from flashlights. There stood six of Leroy's security men, and Leroy was front and center to the rescue.

CHAPTER 49

SECRET REVEALED

"Ishmael, meet your father," Carlos said, laughing.

Leroy was holding his desert eagle with the banana clip and flashlight attached to the end with both hands.

The mayor had called him earlier that night, informing him of what Bowen had in store for Ishmael.

Although in any other situation the mayor would let Bowen take care of problems like Ishmael, this one was different. He felt he owed some type of duty to help Ishmael. Mostly it was the respect he had for Leroy.

Leroy had done so many things for the mayor that no one knew about. Leroy helped him financially when he was disowned by his family many years ago when he'd became strung out on heroin as a teen. After the mayor cleaned himself up, Leroy paid for him to go to college and helped him to get into office, so he sorta owed it to Leroy.

"Fuck is you talking about? That's not my father. You can kiss your ass good-bye now, spic," Ishmael said confidently.

"Hey, Leroy, why don't you tell him?" Carlos said.

"Tell me what?" Ishmael looked at Leroy.

"Let the girl go, Carlos," Leroy belted.

"Leroy, you mean to tell me you haven't told Ishmael?" Carlos continued to smile.

Desiree could feel his grip loosening from around her neck.

"What is he talking about, Leroy?" Ishmael looked at his mentor.

"Tell him, Leroy."

"No you fucking tell me," Ishmael said to Carlos, his patience running out.

"He's your father, Ishmael," Carlos said, laughing.

"What?" Ishmael looked at Leroy.

Leroy would not look him in the eyes. Ishmael felt a twinge in his nuts.

"Is that true, Big Roy?"

Leroy never said a word. He continued to stare at Carlos with piercing eyes.

"Are you my father?" Ishmael asked.

Desiree noticed that Carlos was so involved with their conversation that he had practically lowered the knife. She elbowed Carlos in his stomach as hard as she could and dove to the floor. Carlos rolled to the floor and threw the knife, hitting Ishmael in his calf before he stood. Carlos then reached for his gun.

Leroy and his men opened fire on Carlos, sending him flying into the wall. His body jerked as each piece of hot lead ripped into his flesh. Carlos slid down the wall. His eyes remained opened and seemed to be staring off into the distance.

Ishmael fell to the floor, grabbing his leg. Desiree stood. She wanted to run to his side, but he had betrayed her. He had killed her friends, and she started to feel like maybe he had gotten with her to eventually kill her. Maybe he thought she was going to turn him in for the murders.

Leroy walked over to Ishmael who was grimacing in pain. The huge knife had almost completely imbedded up to the handle into his calf. Leroy ripped off a piece of Ishmael's shirt and instructed one of the men to come over.

The man held his hand out for Ishmael to hold. Ishmael grabbed it with both of his, preparing for the pain that would come when Leroy pulled the knife from his calf.

Leroy yanked the knife out of his leg, and Ishmael screamed in agonizing pain.

Leroy wrapped the piece of cloth around Ishmael's leg, tying it tightly to stop the blood flow.

"Can you get up?" Leroy asked, clearly showing concern and regret.

"Naw," Ishmael stated, breathing heavily.

"Get that chair," Leroy instructed his men, pointing to the chair Desiree had knocked over.

Two of Leroy's men placed Ishmael into the chair. He looked over at Desiree. Her expression showed she was clearly afraid of him. This hurt his heart.

"Leroy, are you my father?" He looked at him seriously.

Leroy stood straight up and stared at him. "Yes, son, I am your father."

Ishmael dropped his head. "Why didn't you tell me?"

"Because I was ashamed, youngun."

"Ashamed? You was ashamed of me? How you sound?"

"Not of you, son, of what I did to conceive you."

"So you knew I was your son yet you still gave me your back?"

"I'm sorry for that, Ishmael, but I'm here for you now."

"Fuck that. You're supposed to be my father, you backstabbing piece of shit. I should blow your fucking brains out right now." He picked up the gun from the floor and pointed it at Leroy who backed up from him.

Leroy's men, cocked and loaded, pointed their weapons at Ishmael.

"Drop it, Ish," one of the men yelled.

"You ain't shit, Leroy. I blamed the wrong man for being my father and it was yo' black-hearted ass. I fucking hate yo' ass." He squeezed the trigger and the bullet whizzed past Leroy's ear, nipping a piece of it off.

Leroy's men opened fire on Ishmael.

"No," Leroy screamed, holding his ear, but it was too late. Ishmael lay on the floor with his foot mounted on the chair, which had fallen with him.

Desiree screamed and began to cry. One of the men grabbed her, and she stood behind the man and cried.

Leroy had tears streaming down his face. Ishmael was his only child, and although Ishmael didn't know it, Leroy did love him.

Ishmael was gasping for air. Blood spilled from his mouth. Leroy sat next to him. He pulled his head into his arms.

"I'm sorry, son," he cried. "I love you."

Ishmael stared up at Leroy and struggled to talk as the blood continued to pour out of his mouth and wounds.

"I know," Ishmael said, taking his last breath.

Thirty minutes later the police arrived at the scene. Leroy in-structed Desiree on what to say to the police. Although she didn't want to go along with it, Leroy did come in to rescue them. Not to mention she saw what type of person Leroy was, and she didn't want to have to run into him ever again, so she cooperated.

The story checked out as far as Damon and Zola. Captain Cohen of the force was dead as well as Bowen. There were seven bodies in one night.

CHAPTER 50

PAYBACK

ONE YEAR LATER

Desiree and Beverly were in her car she had purchased two months before. They had just come back from the long ride to upstate New York. She finally managed to go to the prison where Bilal died. They allowed her to go to his grave, which was located in a field behind the prison walls. She was finally able to get total closure.

Once she reached the city's line, a brown BMW began to follow her. She was so wrapped up in her emotions that she wasn't aware of her surroundings for the first time since the kidnapping. She looked in the rearview mirror and smiled at her infant son, Ishmael Jr., who sat sleeping in his car seat.

They drove down the street to the graveyard that held Ishmael's remains. She had to learn to forgive him in order to move on. He had taken people's lives and two of those lives were her friends, but she still held so much love for the good side of Ishmael in her heart.

Her heart began to race, and her hands began to shake. She turned into the cemetery and stopped at the office to get the location of Ishmael's grave. This would be the first time she had visited it. She missed him so much. If it weren't for Beverly, she might be in an insane asylum.

On that horrible day when Ishmael died, she had gone to Beverly's house. She was too afraid to go home alone. Beverly and her kids came and stayed with her for a few weeks. Beverly was a good friend. She stayed by Desiree's side, encouraging her and holding her when she cried. Later Desiree found out she was carrying Ishmael's child. The experience Desiree went through also rubbed off on Beverly. But Desiree used her pregnancy as a means of holding on. She knew that she never wanted her unborn child to have to go through the life of living in the rough streets of the inner city.

Beverly realized she had told Desiree's whereabouts, which led to her kidnapping. It hurt her to no end. When Desiree forgave her, she knew it was time to change.

Beverly had been a recovering alcoholic of ten months. She was attending school to be a nurse's aide and one day hoped to become a nurse. She was drop-dead gorgeous as long as she didn't open her mouth. Her teeth were still missing and rotten, but she was working on getting dentures.

The women drove in silence as they rounded the curvy road in the cemetery. The brown BMW was about four car lengths back still following them. Desiree parked on the side of the road and turned off the ignition.

"You ready?" she asked Beverly.

"Un-uh, Rae-Rae, not this one. I can't go see Ish's grave," she said as tears filled her eyes. "I'll stay here with Little Ish," she said, looking back at him, smiling.

He was the spitting image of his father. Desiree understood and patted her friend on the hand. "Okay. I'll be back." She grabbed the flowers off the backseat, smiled at her son, and got out of the car to begin the walk up the hill.

She looked at the names as she walked down the row. There it was, Ishmael Willie Jenkins. She walked up to the tombstone and knelt on the freshly mowed lawn. She placed the fresh-cut flowers into the vase that sat in front of the tombstone.

She began to talk to him.

"Hello, Ishmael. I know you think I'm still mad at you, but I'm not. I forgive you, and I still love you very much." Tears filled her eyes as she spoke.

Meantime Beverly sat in the car and stared off into space. She was crying thinking about Ishmael. He was always so nice to her. He helped her whenever she needed it, and he never judged her. If only he could see her now. She was a changed woman, and she knew he would be proud of her.

She smiled to herself when all of a sudden the car door opened abruptly.

Desiree continued to talk to Ishmael and cry. She told him about her finishing school and the great job she had. She told him how he wouldn't believe that Beverly had gotten herself together. She laughed and talked to him like he was sitting right in front of her.

Desiree saw a shadow on the ground. She thought it was Beverly.

"You changed your mind, huh?" Desiree asked as she began to turn around.

"Don't move," a female voice said.

Her heart began to beat two times its normal speed. This couldn't be happening again. She thought about Beverly and hoped she would come to help her.

"What do you want?" she asked in a shaky voice.

"You had the only person I loved more than myself killed," the woman spit with venom in her voice.

"Who? I don't know what you're talking about."

"Yes, you do, bitch," the woman growled.

"Who are you talking about?" Desiree asked with tears running down her face.

"Zola, bitch. My lover. My heart. She was all I had," Nettie yelled, choking back her own tears.

"Zola?"

"Yes, that's right. Zola."

"I swear to you, I didn't know anything about her until that day she died. I'm sorry you lost your...lover, but I didn't have her killed. You have to believe me," Desiree said, panicking. *Where is Beverly?* she thought.

"Have you ever heard that saying revenge is sweet and payback's a bitch?" Nettie asked.

"Yes, please don't hurt me," Desiree begged.

"Too late."

Nettie grabbed a handful of Desiree's hair and pulled her head back so fast that Desiree didn't know what was going on. Nettie spit a razor in her hand and sliced Desiree's neck all in one movement. Desiree fell face first onto Ishmael's grave.

Nettie walked away satisfied with her work. She walked past Desiree's car and looked at Beverly as she lay hanging out of the car with blood pouring from her neck.

Nettie got into her BMW, checked her reflection in the mirror, and smiled at herself. She then looked over at the baby squirming around in the car seat that she had place on the passenger side. Nettie put the pacifier that had fallen out in the infant's mouth then she drove off down the narrow road, not giving a shit if someone saw her or not.

THE END

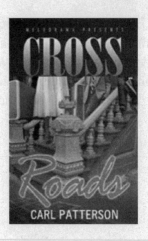

NOW AVAILABLE
FROM THE DESK OF JACKI SIMMONS
STRIPPED

JANUARY 2007
EVA FIRST LADY OF SIN
by STORM

MARK THE DATES!!!
THE CANDY SHOP
FEBRUARY 2007

LIFE AFTER WIFEY
NOVEMBER 2007
by KIKI SWINSON

NOW AVAILABLE
WIFEY

I'M STILL WIFEY

MENACE II SOCIETY
by Al-Saadiq Banks, Mark Anthony, Crystal Lacey Winslow, Isadore Johnson, JM Benjamin

A TWISTED TALE OF KARMA
by AMALEKA G. McCALL

ORDER FORM
(PHOTO COPY)
MELODRAMA PUBLISHING
P.O.BOX 522
BELLPORT, NY 11713
646-879-6315

Please send me the following book(s)
THE CRISS CROSS ISBN: 0-9717021-2-8
WIFEY ISBN: 0-9717021-3-6
I'M STILL WIFEY ISBN: 0-9717021-5-2
A TWISTED TALE OF KARMA ISBN: 0-9717021-4-4
MENACE II SOCIETY ISBN: 0-9717021-7-9
CROSS ROADS ISBN: 0-9717021-8-7
SEX, SIN & BROOKLYN ISBN: 0-9717021-6-0
STRIPPED ISBN: 1-934157-00-7
EVA FIRST LADY OF SIN ISBN: 1-934157-01-5
THE CANDY SHOP 1-934157-02-3
IN MY HOOD ISBN: 0-9717021-9-5

ALL BOOKS ARE PRICED AT $15.00 (u.s.)=_____

QUANTITY: _____

Shipping/Handling* = _____
(*please enclose $3.95 for shipping/handling ($6.00 if order is over $30.00 and under $50.00)

PLEASE ATTACH NAME, COMPLETE MAILING ADDRESS

FOR BULK ORDERS PLEASE CALL THE PUBLISHER OR CONTACT YOUR DISTRIBUTOR.

MAKE ALL CHECKS/MONEY ORDERS PAYABLE TO:
MELODRAMA PUBLISHING